UNDER THE WHISPERING PINES

Gigi John

Please forward all inquiries to UpsidePublishing@gmail.com

The author can be reached by

email @ underthewhisperingpines2022@gmail.com

Instagram @NurseGigi94

Acknowledgements

Gratitude to God Almighty for allowing me to write this book.

Thank you to my Family - Johnny, my loving husband, Pete, Jose and Julie for all their support and encouragement.

A special thank you to Pete for all the time he spent helping me.

Thank you to my parents who are watching over me

All my friends and family for cheering me on

Reeny my baby sister for her encouragement, tips and advice

Ancy, my bestie watching over and rooting for me from Heaven.

Thank you/ Gratitude

Gigi

CHAPTER 1

George leaned against the railing and wept. His chest tightened and the knot in his stomach made him feel queasy. A wave of fear surged inside him. Sweat beads sprouted on his face and trickled down his chin, mixing with a thin stream of tears that ran down his pale, wrinkled cheeks.

Gasping for air he mumbled, "I know she is not coming back, I can't go in and look at her." He turned to Nina and Dolores, who were coming out of Muriel's room carrying soiled linen and depositing them in the dirty utility bin. Dolores took her gloves off, walked up to the sink, and washed her hands with precision. Then she wiped her hands with paper towels as she came back to George and smiled.

"Your beautiful wife is fine. She's sitting on her wheelchair all dolled up, waiting for her George." Dolores said with her usual devilish wink and soothing humor.

She continued, "Muriel gave us a real run for our money this morning." Then she hugged George. "I know, I know you are upset. Muriel has her mood swings. Go in and talk to her. I'll get you a cup of coffee."

Every visit was heartbreaking, but George had made the trip to Whispering Pines every day for the last three years. As hard as the visits were for him, he wanted to see her every day. She had been with him for sixty-eight years, through thick and thin, an inseparable part of his body, his most precious vital organ. Today, he was not sure if his wife saw him, heard him, or felt his presence the way she always had.

On his drive up the hill to Whispering Pines, he often wondered, *Does she know me? Does she sense my presence? Is she waiting for me?* The uncertainty of the answers consumes him with worry as he goes up the winding path.

By the time he parks in the visitor's lot in the front of the building, he knows and reassures himself, *She knows me, she feels me, she waits for me every day. If she doesn't see me she will be heartbroken."*

Dolores handed him a cup of hot, black coffee. "Be careful, it is hot," she reminded him.

George mumbled, "Perfect."

George entered Muriel's room. She sat in her padded wheelchair, breathing heavily. She screamed, "Take me home, take me home. I am going home." She panted, then started screaming again. Her breathing turned into a rattling sound, and, exhausted, she gasped for air. George hurried to the nurse's station.

"Muriel is not well. Please call the doctor."

Elena Maxwell looked at Anna Ritter and shook her head. "As soon as he shows up, she acts out, and he runs to us complaining. When will he realize she is crazy and does not know what she is saying? I don't have time for this shit today." She continued to scan her medication book, flagging the ones for her next medication round.

Anna Ritter, the charge nurse for the day, stood up and walked toward Muriel's room, then turned to Elena and said, "Never! That poor husband will never give up on her." Elena shook her head and buried herself in her chart.

Anna, noticing that Muriel is hot and shivering, tried to calm her. "Look, George is here. Why don't you go to the solarium with George and have a snack? It's snack time." Anna placed her hands around Muriel, who continued to rock and scream.

Dolores came back to the room and helped George wheel Muriel out. Muriel put her legs firmly on the floor and screamed, "No, no, leave me alone."

"Why is she shaking? What is wrong with her? Did you call the doctor?" George asked Anna.

"What is wrong? Something is bothering Muriel," he continued.

No one knew Muriel better than he did, after all.

George left the room and waited while they put Muriel back in bed. Anna came out and told him, "Maybe she has a urinary infection. When Muriel exhibits agitation, she usually has an infection. I will collect some urine and send it for testing. I spoke to Dr Ephraim."

He sighed. He trusted the nurses with Muriel's life and, in a way, his too. They had become his second family within months of Muriel moving in to Whispering Pines. He peeked at Muriel, who was trashing her sheets and trying to get out of bed.

Muriel was a strong woman at heart. She had worked in the school cafeteria scrubbing pots and pans for three decades. She birthed and raised their five children, who all went on to be very successful in life. George and Muriel also have eighteen grandchildren and three great grandchildren! Life was good. They planned to spend the rest of their lives together traveling the world, until reality reshaped their even path. Now they stumble along the cracks and potholes like two weary mules, slipping and sliding with unbearable weight on their backs.

Over the years, the small changes happening in Muriel went unnoticed by family and friends. She was forgetting things. She was getting restless and agitated unpredictably. She left the stove on regularly and wandered from the house a few times, unable to find her way back. She slowly morphs from the voice of reason in the house to the one wreaking pandemonium. George and the kids should have noticed. George beats himself up every minute now for not seeing the changes in his wife.

How could I not see what was happening?

At the time, George had ignored the changes he saw and rationalized them as normal signs of aging.

At seventy-three, are we old? Do we change over to a different person? When does our brain take a twist to forgetfulness?

When the children visited, they did not see the tousled, unkempt hair, wrinkled, smelly clothes, and untidy kitchen. The odor emanating from their mother was overlooked. To children, parents never change.

At the synagogue she was quieter, as if fighting to hide her true self.

As the days passed by, her eyes started to plead, *Help me*, but who noticed that? No one! Everyone around turned a blind eye to reality, only seeing what they wanted to see.

She was always the perfect neighbor, wife, and mother. When she started to fall apart mentally, showing it through her appearance and behavior, none of her loved ones noticed anything odd.

She's their wife and mother, she does not change. How could she?

Maybe she is tired!

Maybe the hormones!

The retirement!

It is not humanly possible to perceive that anything is wrong with her.

Muriel was not bedraggled in front of neighbors, only family.

To George, the twists and turns in her behavior appeared, over time, to be kind of normal. He ignored practical unobserved and unseen facts presumptuously. She had been both his left and right hand through their struggles in life. He believed she was entitled to act out a little in their home. All of the craziness amused him. If there was anything wrong, the children, or at least their spouses, would have pointed it out, he rationalized.

Muriel's tangled mind and body was tightening, and she felt a discord in her being. Unable to express it, she became angrier and more frustrated. She screamed out, but her cries for help fell on deaf ears.

George remembered the day he was waiting at the bank with Muriel. They were in line to cash a check when she started to get restless. She looked at George and started to hit him with her pocketbook. George smiled and kissed her on the cheek. To him, this was not unusual. When he could not console her as she continued to hit him, George tried to haul her out of the bank, gently tugging her hands, without drawing the attention of bystanders.

Muriel pushed George aside and ran inside a conference room where bank employees were having a meeting. She screamed and started attacking them, scratching them with her nails and hitting them left and right with her pocketbook. She showered them with profanities. George had never heard her use any obscene words in all the years he had known her.

The bank officials called 911, and she was taken to the emergency room of the nearest hospital. When they arrived, Muriel did not remember any part of the incident. The psychiatrist bombarded George with question after question, but George only responded, "I don't know. Please wait for my son. He is on his way."

George Jr. was the first of their five children to arrive. He was followed by Anika who was wiping tears, frantic about her mother.

"Is Mother having a heart attack, a stroke? Daddy, what is it?"

George shook his head. "I don't know."

Tommy, Isabel, and Mabel arrived together. They stood still and quiet next to George, not daring to ask anything for fear of a worse diagnosis.

The nurse poked her head out and asked for the family of Muriel. Everyone motioned George Jr. to go inside as their proxy. After three and a half hours of waiting outside in fear and uncertainty, they could wait a bit longer. Isabel held on to her father with all her might. He stroked his daughter's hand and said, "All is fine baby." His voice had lost its poignant undertone, which worried her more.

His face said, *I don't know baby!*

George Jr. came out after meeting with the doctor, faced his family, and said, "They have to admit her and do a battery of tests. They are unsure what is going on. Can I authorize the tests for you, Dad? There are some forms to be filled out too."

George nodded, "Yes."

Isabel, Tommy, Anika, and Mabel agreed with their father.

When they got to see her, Muriel was calm and asleep on top of crisp white sheets. The nurse explained there was an alarm on her bed for safety, if she woke up suddenly and tried to get out of bed.

"Why?" asked Isabel.

The nurse responded with a question of her own. "Have you noticed the bruises on her body? That is typical of multiple falls."

She continued, "Have you ever witnessed any falls?"

"No," they answered in unison. Their bewildered voices resonated inside the hospital room.

The nurse continued, "People try to hide their shortcomings in the beginning stages of memory loss. They are conscientious of their shortcomings, hence the odd behavior, agitation, anger, and unpredictable outbursts."

"What nonsense is she talking about? There is nothing wrong with mom." Anika said to her father as the nurse left the room.

"You are absolutely right. Your mom remembers everything. Just yesterday she was talking about the first time we went out on a date. She had all the specifics that I had forgotten."

The family wanted to take her home immediately. How dare anyone say their Muriel is crazy?

Several tests later, Dr. Richard Khan called them into his office.

The words advanced dementia did not sink in clearly for the family.

George said, "So what? Who is not forgetful, especially at her age?"

Dr. Khan explained, "Keeping Muriel safe should be your number-one priority. That means you have to look for placement in a facility that specializes in caring for people with dementia." He tried to read into their puzzled eyes and shocked faces. There was disbelief, anger, and tears plastered over the six faces staring at him.

The doctor continued, "Muriel will stay in the hospital for another day or two. If you have any questions, please feel free to call me. I will have the psychiatrist consult with her also. The case manager could help you with the placement or home stay. It is up to you. Please go home and discuss your options."

At home, Mabel and Anika went into their mother's closet. The smell of dirty clothes shocked them. It was so unlike their mother, who was neat and organized all the time.

"Didn't Dad see this?" Anika whispered to Mabel. Mabel shook her head in disbelief.

George poured a shot of jack, took a swig, and started to recount incident after incident that he had ignored at the time. There was the time when Muriel could not find her way home and drove around the neighborhood until one of the neighbors found her.

Muriel's unprovoked outbursts at George and the kids!

One Sunday dinner, Muriel's famous marble cake tasted salty. Everyone joked and laughed about it, and she laughed with them. Isabel and Tommy brought out ice cream for the kids as dessert in place of the marble cake.

Family and friends had complained that she was not answering or returning their calls.

The messy house, clothes, and various strange incidents seemed to paint a picture now.

How could it be? How could we not see it? George sighed.

He saw his children sitting together and talking among themselves. He joined them.

"How could all of us overlook the changes in Mom? How could we miss it?" Isabel wept

George said, "She is your mother. How could any of us think she is ill? We couldn't!"

Tommy, always the voice of reason in the family, said, "Let's get a second opinion and go from there."

No one ate dinner. No one slept. The five children and their father just held each other. Their spouses gave them the space to process, digest, and come up with a healthy solution together.

George stretched out in his armchair. In the darkness of night, sparkling memories of happiness and sorrow passed through his mind, tickling his senses to reach an ultimate goal. *How can we keep her safe?*

In the wee hours of the morning, he got up. The weary siblings rolled up or stretched out in the living room made him feel sadder. "They need their mother."

George made coffee and, one by one, they entered the kitchen. George said, "I am going to meet with the case manager today. You cannot put your life on hold and suffer through more stress and pain than is necessary. Our priority is to keep Mom safe. I should have known better."

"Dad," Anika tried to protest, but George waved his hand.

"It is okay, honey. Your mother took care of us all these years and it is our turn now. We have to do right by her."

He couldn't stay longer without bursting into tears in front of his kids. He hurried outside and started tending to the garden to release his frustration, anger, and sorrow.

"Muriel's paranoia and agitation is getting worse," the social worker told George and George Jr.

She suggested twenty-four-hour care at home, or placement in a specialized dementia facility. George felt disconnected and dumfounded as he was flooded with a parade of questions about Muriel's present state of mind.

"Can you help us with any changes you noted recently?" The social worker stared at him.

George read her thoughts, *Yeah, as if he paid attention! Another senile old man barely managing.*

Junior was realistic, "None of us saw any changes in Mom. Maybe we never noticed. Definitely nothing unusual."

George was against keeping her institutionalized. He was devastated. Sleepless nights, agonizing minutes, the children talking to him, and George trying to comfort them in vain. What a nightmare! It was an unexpected twist, sloping down into a chasm of uncertainty, a sudden role reversal for George. Now he had to tend to all that Muriel used to do. He decided on twenty-four-hour homecare. They had money stashed aside for rainy days, and the rain was here.

After three days of homecare, Muriel chased the caregiver out of the house, accusing her of stealing valuables and poisoning Muriel's food.

She screamed, "Get out before I call the police."

George was powerless. He could not instill reality into her recalcitrant brain.

George Jr and Anika came with George to visit facilities recommended by the social worker. The ambiance, aura, and the general feeling made them feel satisfied with their choice of Whispering Pines. Under the present circumstances, this was the best choice for Muriel, they all agreed. And off she went to Whispering Pines with its winding path, weeping willows, and mighty pine trees behind the gray walls guarding the Hudson.

George saw Agatha wheeling her husband, Simon, to the recreation room and followed them. The residents were getting ready to play Bingo. He helped the employees and volunteers arrange the game. An hour had passed before he even thought about Muriel. This had become part of his routine, finding reasons to stay around, some days until dusk. He made friends with other family members, residents, volunteers, and employees. It made him feel safe to linger around Muriel. He felt her presence in his every fiber, a feeling of completeness, and he savored every bit of it. George tried to hold on to it as long as he could.

Placing Muriel at Whispering Pines was an emotional relief for George. He had time to de-stress, rejuvenate, and be with Muriel at the same time. The children frequently reminded him that their choice was appropriate. Muriel was safe!

Maria Murphy passed by, mumbling,
Destiny is not a matter of chance
It is a matter of choice
It is not something to be waited for
But rather something to be achieved.
She wandered the hallway aimlessly. Linda Crawford, wheeling the medication cart, halted in front of Maria.

"Miss Murphy, I have your vitamins."

Maria ignored Linda and kept walking. George watched her.

If the nurse insisted, Maria could be thrown into one of her violent mood changes, which ended up in aggressive behaviors.

    Maria continued,

    One's destination is never a place

    But rather a new way of looking at things.

Agatha and George nodded at each other. Simon slept in his chair. They were people with new vision, who accepted their life as it was today, meeting the demands and challenges thrown at them at odd moments, yet content while making the best of it. Simon never uttered a word.

CHAPTER 2

On a cloudy, gray summer afternoon, Hal Blum sat in the lounge chair behind the patio door facing the Hudson. He wiggled his body to sink deeper into the cushion until he felt cozy. He sighed as the little task—to make himself comfortable—was accomplished.

Every uptight cell and molecule in his brain relaxed. The clouds hovering over Whispering Pines stepped aside in the sky. Hal smiled. The tight muscles relentlessly wrestled a faint smile on the corner of his lips. The scar on his chin from his tour in Vietnam grew wider.

Nothing much to think about or do, he stretched out his hands behind his head. The pines bordering the Hudson were thick, as they usually were in spring and early summer. He strained to look at the highway behind the Hudson and the ongoing traffic. From where he sat, the vehicles on the highway looked like a cluster of slow-moving ants in different shapes and shades.

The yachts and speed boats zig zagged rhythmically on the waves. Their pace was occasionally slashed by a big boat racing past them. The river, in its elegance, embraced it all. The waves hugged and caressed every one of them.

Maria Murphy often spoke about the way the Hudson rustled the minds of onlookers.

The Canadian ducks were flying in unison parallel to the pines fencing the building. The weeping willows bowed their heads as the flock of birds passed them. Their synchronized movements formed an arch in the sky. Hal closed his eyes, embracing it all.

He opened his eyes when Maria walked past him while Dolores followed behind, calling her name.

The serenity he had created for himself was disrupted by intruding noises.

Then his gaze moved to the highway.

Where are they going? Who might be in the cars? His thoughts strayed. *Are they safe? Is there anyone trying to hurt them?*

What did I do?

Will I hurt them?

Am I safe?

Forgotten memories erupted inside Hal's fragile mind. A spark ignited.

Hal Blum jumped up from his chair and started pacing. As his mind started to roar at a tumultuous pace, his feet moved faster. Soon he was sweating profusely.

The highway in front of him transformed into the streets of Vietnam, ricocheted with memories hiding in the deep recesses of his mind. He covered his ears. The cries of pleading women and weeping children in pools of blood erupted in front of him. The sound of boots on stone-paved paths plagued his soul.

The fear, torment, and guilt of an era sent shivers down his spine. Sweaty and shaking, he ran inside. He stopped at the nurse's station.

Elizabeth Mann was transcribing orders after Dr. Ephraim left the unit. Piles of papers and heaps of charts were scattered in front of her.

Blum screamed, "I am scared. Help me, help me. I molested women. I killed, I killed." Panting and shivering, he continued, "I hurt people. God, I don't remember what I did!"

Hal pulled his hair and growled. "What did I do? Why did I do all that?"

Elizabeth stood up. "Okay, Hal. I am coming to help you." She pushed aside her work and dashed in Hal's direction with a steady pace and calm demeanor. She did not want to provoke any repercussions or to add to his trepidation.

No one around Hal could cope with his dysphoria at its

worst, especially the anxious patients consumed in their own perceived normalcy. A slight tilt could unbalance their whole thought process and cause irrational behavior.

Elizabeth wanted to de-escalate the situation before Hal lost total control of himself and his relentless surge of repressed emotions surfaced. Next there would be monstrous voices screaming, Hal punching the object next to him and falling down on the floor, weeping his heart out.

Some of the residents crossing his path in the past have been hurt. The joke at the nurse's station is, "Don't mess up with Hal, he will hex you down." Staying away from his wrath is not an easy task. Elizabeth knew better. She could always sense the storm brewing in the Atlantic and shifting along the Hudson to Whispering Pines.

"Let's take a walk," Elizabeth extended her right hand and held Hal's hand. Her left hand gently touched his shoulder. Non-threatening approach and soothing touch.

"Breathe, Elizabeth, breathe, Cleansing breaths! Okay, you are good." She heard Mrs. Baker whispering to her.

Hal struck her hands away from him. He was already in a place where he pictured himself as a pervert, a molester, a brutal executioner, and he kept chanting, "I lived in sin. I molested women. What do I do know? I am in hell."

His shaking body bent over to the floor. He wept, his face in his hands. His sobbing was loud enough to get the attention of Guiseppina, who was walking past the nurse's station.

A staunch Catholic, she said, "God forgives."

Hal Blum looked up and screamed, "Go away, Ginny, mind your own business. Or else I will make you."

Guiseppina dashed at Hal Blum, her fingers waving at his face, "Vaffanculo."

Linda came out and said, "Okay, okay, let's go."

She approached Guiseppina and steered her away from Blum. Guiseppina obliged until she reached the corner of the corridor, where she turned and shouted, "Figlio di puttana."

"Guiseppina, what would your children say if they heard

you?" Linda asked

"Soap in their mouth. Slap, slap," Guiseppina replied.

"I think you need soap and a slap now," Linda laughed.

Guiseppina, safely seated back in her room, was mumbling inaudibly.

The intensity of his rational and irrational emotions coated in guilt and sorrow weighed heavily on Hal Blum. Linda called two of the CNAs Douglas Chester and Charles Walter. "We need to get Blum to the solarium, and I want one of you to stay with him until he is calm."

Hal was not a fan of Charles, but Hal obliged when Doug said, "Hey, Hal, I am going to the solarium. It's snack time. Want to come?"

He nodded.

"Breathe in and out. That is what I do when my daughter riles me up," Doug said, and winked. "Mr. Blum, you will be fine, I know for sure."

Dr. Ephraim used to say, watching Hal and Charles, "I think they were husband and wife in a former life. I think Hal was the Mrs. No wonder he hates Charles for no reason."

Hal got off the floor and started to walk with Doug.

"How old is your daughter?" Hal asked.

Elizabeth looked at Charles and Linda. They laughed in unison.

"Does he have a daughter?"

Elizabeth Mann shook her head.

"All is well," Doug called out.

The dark cloud hovering over Hal Blum receded as he felt comforted by the staff. His memories and recriminating thoughts vanished. His mind set on nourishment, he went into the solarium with long, steady strides, holding hands with Douglas Chester.

"Thank you, Dougie," the nurses called out. They had dodged Hal's meltdown with ease of practice. Though it was not always the case. As time passed, they had learned what worked for each of their residents. The staff was familiar with their naughty traits, and they had antidotes for each one of them. Blum always responded to food.

Elizabeth wanted to redirect Hal's mind to a happy place where he could stay in peace, and Doug made it possible. She sighed, ignored the paper piles, and walked into the day room. Minty Weinberg waved at Elizabeth and smiled, chocolate dripping from the corner of her upper lip. She was having a chocolate cookie that Charles gave her, although she was on the list for a diabetic gelatin cup for snack. Elizabeth wriggled her nose and pointed her fingers at Charles, "You are going to be in big trouble, mister. Her blood sugar climbs through the roof."

Charles looked at Elizabeth, "Hey Liz, do you want Minty to be a good girl? Anyway, she takes insulin. What difference does it make if her sugar is a little spiky?"

Elizabeth nodded. "I would want a drink, a real one! if it were me."

George joined in and laughed, "Me, too, sweetheart. Let me know when."

These were the moments of sanity mingled with laughter and soothing words of consolation to carry them all forward when no one thinks there is hope.

George sat next to John Schafer, Agatha, and Simon. He saw Constance adjusting Annabel's bib. Lisa and Cynthia repositioned Albert Crowly, who forgets to move without help. The room was getting more active, as Louise Martin walked in and lingered at the door.

Charles called, "Louise, over here." He pulled a chair out for her.

She said, "Thank you."

Dolores brought Minnie in, and she sang under her breath as she walked in wearing her black heels and asked Doug, "What can I do, Master?"

Dolores said, "Just listen to music and have a snack."

Ruth Fisher was sitting with her daughter-in-law, Francine. Ruth was cursing and scolding Francine for stealing her only son from her and, above all, leaving her institutionalized.

Victoria Steward came up and said, "Miss Fisher, can I take you to the toilet?"

She replied, "Why can't this gold digger bitch do it? She stole my son." Her voice gained ground as she saw she had an audience.

Victoria motioned Francine to leave the room, who mouthed a silent thank you as she went. Francine gathered Ruth's dirty clothes to take home to wash and stopped at the nurse's station to say goodbye.

"So, what is Mama up to today?" asked Linda Crawford.

"She was the nicest person until the dementia. We were so close. I don't know where all this hatred and anger is coming from. She does not have a bad bone in her body," Francine said.

"Well, they say the darnedest things. That is the beauty of it. I think all the repressed feelings surface as the brain shrinks. They are given a free pass, a free license to shoot out what they feel like, not exactly unintentional or maybe intentional, who knows?" Linda said.

Elizabeth interjected, "I want to stick it to some people. If I do it now I will lose my job and license."

"Wait for a little while. You will end up here," Lisa Mosley, passing by with a stack of clean white sheets, said.

"Count me in, too," Francine laughed, and left.

George waited in the solarium, giving Muriel time to rest. Charles poured him another cup of coffee. This was getting to be his daily routine, spending time around Muriel and helping the staff as much as he could. Muriel, his life, was here. These people took care of her. They were honestly vested in his interests, too. They laughed with him, they cried with him. Such a give and take for him and the staff.

George was always supportive, and an ardent advocate for the staff. When families accused the staff of wrongdoings, George, Mrs. Schafer, and Francine volunteered to buffer those situations.

George drifted off in a haze. He swam inside the hidden caves of memory he had stashed away. He occasionally delved into those hidden caves and came out with grief for his losses. Sometimes he was tickled with the joys of days gone by and blessed moments captured in the realms of his memory.

Has Muriel stored those memories?

He will never know. For the past eighteen months, she hadn't uttered a sane word that made sense to him.

What is left?

Although his kids could disagree, he silently pined over his losses. They were his losses! They still had family dinner once a week in his house. Everyone seemed to settle into the routine as it became the new norm. Deep down, George couldn't help but feel Muriel's absence. The noise and smell of food when his family came over was a welcome change to his lonely evenings. He knew it was no more than a cheap, soothing balm on his open wound. In between his thoughts of Muriel, he played with his grandchildren and great-grand children, smiled, and conversed with the adults as he made it through the evening.

Isabel, his youngest daughter, packed and labelled food for George. She made sure the pantry was well stocked with his favorite items. Isabel was the reincarnation of Muriel. She was always the first to come and the last to leave. She tried to organize everything in order for her dad as her mother had in the past.

One solace George had was that the kids were busy with their lives. Their jobs and families kept them too busy to focus on Muriel as often as George did. He felt most lonely at night, after he returned from Whispering Pines to an empty home.

Isabel stands reluctantly in the driveway every time she visits her father, anguish on her face. She would never leave until George walked up to her and nudged her forehead, "Get going before the Sunday traffic hits." He then drowned his sorrow in a shot of Jack, neat. He is left alone to his deepest thoughts of anguish and despair, until the phone rings to let him know that the kids and their families are safe at their abodes. The last call, as usual, is from Isabel.

George was interrupted while taking a stroll down memory lane by Louise Martin bumping into him. With her blank stare, she looked at George. George got up and helped her to a chair. Louise never talked, except when her grandchildren visited. She laughed and she talked then, but as soon as they left she shut down her mind. Her blank stare allowed her to count the days and nights until her grandchildren visited again.

What power has the mind over our body? Why is Louise Martin's mind and body content with what she has become?

She has patterned herself into a life of quietness. The staff were amazed at the fact that she never laughed or cried, she was never agitated, and she always wore the blank stare on her face, as if she were locked up in oblivion. Celine Mathews, the night shift charge nurse, often said, "Lou listens to the depth of silence. What a gift!"

George wished he were like Louise.

But who could say what she was actually feeling?

George walked back to Muriel's room. *She might be awake by now.*

Muriel was sleeping when George came back to the room. He sat in the chair by the side of her bed without waking her. He dozed off. Another day inching to dusk, carrying the heavy hearts of many as Whispering Pines got ready for nighttime routines.

CHAPTER 3

Maria Murphy wandered away from the solarium. She was mumbling, "Where can I find true love, love deep and pure?" She could make up a poem out of the blue, in an instant. Words flowed out of her like a spring.

Then she started to look around, as if searching for a lost object. It was amazing that Maria Murphy, the ninety-two-year-old retired teacher was able to recite poems from any book she had ever read or taught. As a high school teacher, she taught English literature, mainly poetry.

Maria saw George and nodded. She stopped in front of Muriel's room

"Hey, Maria," George said.

Maria looked straight at George, then looked around and walked past the room, humming

How many loved your moments of glad grace,
And loved your beauty with false or true;
But one man loved the pilgrim soul in you,
And love the sorrows of your changing face.

George stared in disbelief. It was as if WB Yeats had summed up his life!

Maria held onto the side rails and waited. What is she waiting for? She said, "Can any of you recite when you are old?"

With no response from staff or onlookers, Maria tried to find the next words, but failed to remember the rest of the poem. She started to get agitated—she could not remember the rest. She stepped on the ground with force, tugged at her dress, and screamed. Lisa Mosley was in charge of the solarium at that time. She called Elizabeth and asked her to get someone to help her. She was not allowed to leave the solarium until she had a relief staff member take over.

"Maria is going to fall," Lisa said.

George stretched out his hand and Maria took it. He said gently, "Can you recite the rest? You know, I was really bad in poetry. Maybe it would have been different if you were my teacher."

Maria leaned against the wall and looked at George. She smiled

And bending down beside the glowing bars,
Murmur, a little sadly, how love fled
And paced upon the mountains overhead,
And hid his face amidst a cloud of stars.

Maria sighed. The loss of love in her life, which was a mystery to her whole family, sacred and hidden away in her heart, made her sad. George shook his head, *As if love never goes away. Entangled and intertwined thoughts of the past!* Maria turned back, going with George to the solarium, to safety.

Victoria Stewart, who had rushed in to help, let out a sigh of relief and remarked, "It is the full moon, Georgie." George smiled, nodded, and then proceeded to collect the paper cups, plastic spoons, and crumpled napkins scattered around on tabletops, on the floor, and on the laps of sleeping residents, as evening snack time had ended.

Lisa Mosley walked around, cleaning hands and faces, and tidying the room as she moved from resident to resident, peaking at the clock with discretion and anticipation to be relieved of this duty in thirty minutes. She guided Mr. Blum to use the restroom. "Thank you, George," Lisa said. "What will we do without you?" She laughed and George joined her. So did Constance, sinking into a sense of relief and gratitude that lasted for just seconds.

Minnie wandered off, immersed in her own world, constricted by her past and what was left of it.

At seven, music therapy entertained the residents. They chose music that could hack into their frozen layers, revealing flashes of bygone memories. Memories—good and bad, fond and harsh—flooded like torrential rain and at times like a gentle breeze to ruffle the silence erupting between bewildering moments. Michele Schuler, the music therapist, swore by the power of music to rekindle memories. She practiced relaxation music therapy. As therapeutic as it sounded, George remembered a conversation with her when she told him that she had a doctorate and her research theme was about the positive influence of music in people with dementia.

By the time Michele walked in with her guitar, it was five past seven and John Schafer was restless and shouting. "You, you, you, are late." He was an accountant by profession and his world revolved around numbers. He was trying to get out of the lounge chair. He wanted to say more, but he got choked up in his emotions. He mumbled again, "Say, say, say." He was getting to a state that would lead him to bouts of screaming and yelling.

"John, come with me." George left Maria and walked up to him, taking him outside for a walk. Constance sat quietly and observed the room, half-dazed from the evening medications in her system.

Constance, unable to think, asked herself, *How can I ever be Constance again?*

Constance Angeline Sutton rose from her chair and walked up to Mr. Blum, who came back and sat down, mumbling, "What can I do, killing, killing, all the killing."

Constance touched him gently on his shoulder. When he turned around and looked at Constance, she said "It is okay." Hal looked in her eyes and her calm demeanor transferred a deep sigh of relief as he leaned back in his chair. Constance sat next to him and rested her left hand on his shoulder. The gentle feel of warmth on his skin! His tense muscles started to loosen. George smiled at them. Constance and Hal held hands and sang along with Michele.

Take me out to the ball game,
Take me out with the crowd;
Buy me some peanuts and Cracker Jack.

George watched Constance and wondered, *If Mr. Sutton was alive, what would he say? Maybe he is turning restlessly in his grave, unable to come out and take Constance away from Whispering Pines with him!*

George knew that Mr. Sutton was a millionaire and philanthropist. George said to himself, *If I had that kind of money, Muriel would be at home with me. Well, if she did not chase the caretakers out of the house. She could be home now. She cannot move without help. She cannot talk intelligently. All she does is scream.*

Constance laughed, thinking about Jack Norworth and Albert Von Tilzer waltzing in Heaven, happily proud of their song serving such therapeutic splendor and calmness inside the gray walls of commotion.

Life draws concrete pictures that we understand and then abstract ones that keep us guessing and wondering. George theorized; *Life is art."*

"Time to go home," George walked back to Muriel's room. He quietly took his hat and the bag containing Muriel's dirty laundry, gently kissed her on her forehead, and left the room.

The nurses waved at him on his way out.

"Hang in there, George. See you tomorrow," said Linda Crawford.

"Thank you for your help, sugar," Elizabeth called out.

"Good night, honey," Mirna waved.

"George, have a drink on me," Dolores hugged him. He wrapped himself in the warm embrace, the empathy, and the closeness he felt to each of them.

Miss Ruby scolded Dolores, "What are you talking about drinking, Dolores? It's the devil's work." She was filling in for an evening shift.

"Here we go," the nurses burst into laughter. George laughed and left. As he drove down the spiral road he sighed. "Another day." During the drive back down the winding hill to the main road, he changed his thought process.

She did not know I was there. I don't know if she knew I was next to her for all that time. I don't know if she felt my touch!

George merged into the oncoming traffic on the freeway.

At home, he sat in his lounge chair, sipping whiskey and

reminiscing fond thoughts of their lives together, thoughts which are dear to him.

Loneliness and distress from the brutal collection of past memories! They floated away as if from a dream, shifting to fear and uncertainty. The harder you try to recall the dream, the more vague it becomes! Swirling in chaos and sinking to the bottom of it all, George sipped his drink, neat and dry.

CHAPTER 4

Constance wondered, "Is it getting cooler in the Hamptons?"

She came to Whispering Pines in July. She remembered feeling the New York summer heat while they carried her inside the building from the ambulance. She was drowsy, half-conscious, fading in and out of reality. She was in a hazy cloud of forgetfulness from the medications she was given before being discharged from the hospital. No wonder all she vaguely remembered was the weather. It was four weeks since she became a resident of Whispering Pines.

The Hudson River, in all her might, lay by the side of Whispering Pines. Constance saw men and women sitting on benches under the wide sprawl of majestic pine trees looming around the gray building, the gentle breeze, the waves in the water, and the chattering birds flying above them! It was a perfect summer day! Constance watched the little girl with the ponytail and pink shorts running back and forth, collecting twigs from the ground and throwing them in the Hudson. Constance smiled, and her lips hid aches of a forsaken past, little girls in ponytails running around making her beam with joy.

Constance sighed and decided to take a stroll in the backyard. She stopped to tell the administrative assistant at the nurse's station that she would be outside. The nurses needed to know where everyone was at all times for the safety of the residents.

Rules are rules, she told herself, *even for Constance Angeline Sutton!*

Inhaling the humidity combined with the breeze from the Hudson, Constance walked along the paved pathway. She discretely eyed the families visiting their loved ones. Some of the residents recognized their loved ones, others were in total oblivion of visiting family and friends. But they kept on coming —children, spouses, nieces, nephews, neighbors, and whoever was in their past lives.

It seemed like she was the only one without a visitor. Constance smiled and waved at the girl with the ponytail and pink shorts. She ran to her mother, hid her face in her lap, and, after a moment, turned her face to see if Constance was still standing there. Constance stopped when she was near the river and sat down on a wooden bench.

The gentle breeze tumbled her curls. Constance drew her fingers through her hair.

When was my hair professionally done last?

Who knows!

She looked into the river. She spotted fishing rods protruding from dry fences. The short waves were merciful to the jet skiers and boats, a contrast to the waves she used to enjoy from the porch of her Hamptons bungalow. When the sea was calm, she surfed and sunbathed on the private beach, which stretched out with beautiful sand. The smooth mornings with gentle tides were exceptional. Henry and Constance, hand in hand, striding after a morning cup of coffee! This was the time Henry usually confided his joys, plans, fears, and hopes to Constance. Sometimes pretending to be an ardent listener, she was really looking for shells and oddly shaped stones, beaten up by the raging sea and finally taking refuge on the Hampton shore.

In spite of her "Yes, sweetie" and "Really?," Henry would eye her and, when he knew she was immersed in her collections and not in him, he would tackle her to the smooth sand and say, "Really," staring into her green eyes.

They rolled on the wet and dry sand, laughing. Finally, exhausted, they would stay still and dream, looking at the clear sky.

Did he ever mention that he would leave me, and was he aware of what our precious children planned for their mother?

What a condescending jab! Henry's foresight did not envision this for his wife.

When was I last there? Two weeks before Henry died, on a cold winter day in March.

They had strolled hand in hand. Henry had an unusual glow around his firm lips. He did not say much. Constance felt a surge of unspoken words rush out in his touch. Words still gushing up to be spit out, but right now she has no place that will let her listen to them. The one who used to listen to her vanished forever from her life, but still lingers in her soul. The haunting unbroken silence!

What was Henry thinking when they walked together for the last time?

She planned to spend a few days at the end of August in the Hamptons. Maybe she could spend hours daydreaming, maybe read a book, maybe knit a blanket and bring it back to one of the residents. First she will have the blanket blessed by the minister. Her healing blankets have provided warmth and comfort to many in the past. She has to consult Anthony, her chauffeur, and Martha, Anthony's daughter, who is a lawyer now. Martha tends to her like a daughter. Ebony, Anthony's wife, has to come too. She was her housekeeper for twenty-one years. Constance knew they would arrange any day for her convenience.

A week in the Hamptons with all three of them would be good for her. She has to inform the social worker about her plan first. It won't be a problem because of her financial status. She is private pay! Gee! She smiled. She has a well-furnished one bedroom at Whispering Pines, for which her children donated and paid generously. They wanted Mom to be comfortable at Whispering Pines! She wanted to tell each one of her children, "Be happy your father is not around."

The thought brought tears to her eyes. Her chest heaved and became tight. Abysmal sorrow permeated inside, choking her. A chill slithered through her spine and left her shivering. She held on to the railing of the bench for support and tried hard to breathe. The harder she tried, the more she choked and panicked. Finally she felt numb and calm. Then she took slow, steady breaths, and that brought color back to her face.

It did not matter to her children if she was happy or content with her current life. It mattered to them to have the mansion in Westchester, the financial holdings and assets to themselves.

Why did they ever think I would stand in their way?

Sophia, her only daughter, sided with her three brothers in court to prove that their mother had dementia and she was unable to stay by herself. They could prove that she refused help from her children. What a coincidence when two doctors testified in court about her mental instability. She was institutionalized by her tearful children, who vowed to protect her from any harm.

Life had taken many turns, for the best, for the worst, and now this! Without Henry, she was left to bear it all by herself. A ray of melancholy entered into her mind and thoughts as she wandered through her past.

The pine cones scattered on the ground and rolled over. The pine needles were swaying in the breeze from the Hudson. The person who named this place might have been really prudent. When the wind wandered through the pines, it seemed like they were whispering. Whispering pines among the weeping willows! Seems to be complicated, like the lives under the roof of this institution, not only for the residents but also for everyone connected to them!

All her life she held her four children under her spread wings and kept them safe. Ed Cohen, her lawyer, was ready for a fight when he came to know what they had orchestrated. He visited her to get the process started, but Constance refused.

"Please let me do this. What your kids have done to you is reprehensible," Ed pleaded.

"No, I won't," Constance remained stubborn.

"Well, what would Henry say?" Ed continued.

"Henry isn't here, is he?" Constance shook her head and walked away.

What use is it to fight her own children and cause more heartache and pain? She had been here for thirty-one days now. The first week, she was still in cloudy haze from the medications she had been given since Henry died. She was told those pills were for sleep.

As Dr. Newman had put it, "Just a low dose, for sleep."

After Henry died, Sophia stayed with her at home until Constance was placed at Whispering Pines. On the day she was admitted, the Hudson served as a backdrop to an inauspicious reality.

Sophia whispered, "Charles, William, and Edward researched the place thoroughly, and Whispering Pines is the most beautiful place available. You will get a private room overlooking the Hudson." The gray building looked like a ghost in the summer sun. Sophia exclaimed, "Awesome."

Constance was stunned and confused. She heard Sophia conference call her brothers and her husband. Constance watched Sophia shaking hands with people in suits and some in uniforms. A host of people came in the room and introduced themselves, her clothes were unpacked, and pictures arranged on the nightstand. Dolores Cooper and Nina Hughes had helped Sophia unpack Constance's belongings. Sophia opened her wallet, but even before she pulled out any money Nina grabbed her gently and said, "Please, we do not take any money. Thank you."

Dolores stated, "We love our jobs. You could bring us goodies and leave 'em at the nurse's station for all of us, if you really insist on doing something."

"Stop it Dolores, I am on Weight Watchers. We have free Weight Watchers at our job. Going on week two," Nina argued, and burst out laughing with Dolores. Sophia joined them. The staff was trying hard to make the transition easy on all of them.

Sophia hugged them both and profusely thanked them. She turned to Constance, "Mom, smile for picture of the first day of the new chapter in your life. I will send it to the boys. They will be happy if they see you are happy."

Constance stirred and looked at her with wide, glazed eyes. She tried to fathom the moment.

The vagueness! What is happening? My child wants a picture of their "Confused, harmful to self and others Mother, in an institution!

For what? To mock and laugh or to ease their conscience! Rage took over.

Constance took the picture of her family from the nightstand and threw it straight at Sophie. She doesn't remember if hitting Sophie was her intention or if it was a blind throw, letting out her frustration and wrath. Her children wanted to memorialize their mother's first day in an asylum with a photograph? The picture frame hit Sophie's forehead, and she started to bleed. This was evidence that she was violent and unsafe. Score one! Witnesses who watched the scene nodded, as if it was normal behavior for Constance.

"Relax, it is kind of normal in most patients," Dolores told Sophie.

Employees, residents, and some visitors peeked around curiously. Constance was ecstatic with anger, fear, and, worst of all, a state of helplessness. The only thing she did not feel was remorse about hurting Sophie. The feeling of helplessness wore her down. She was always in control of her actions. Not now. Maybe, not anymore.

In utter despair she screamed, "The hell with you crazy offspring."

She was held down, and soon she felt the pinch of a needle and a burning sensation. She stumbled into a state of frenzy, unable to speak her mind anymore. She heard Maria outside, quoting Milton.

"Confusion worse confounded."

Is it not reality! It was there from Genesis—the first offspring breaking Eve's heart. Betrayal, jealousy, and confusion ruled. Constance saw people hugging and consoling Sophie before her eyes turned cloudy while vague shadows clustered around her. The shattered defiance on her face faded away as she heard Maria's voice outside.

The night hath come; it is no longer day?
The night hath not yet come
Cut off from labor by the failing light
Some work remains for us to do and dare

Even the oldest tree some fruit may bear
And as the evening twilight fades away
The sky is filled with stars invisible by day.

Constance remembered reading Longfellow. What a coincidence that, in her utter despair, Maria shed some light into reality. With no ammunition in her possession to fight back, she closed her eyes and fell into a deep, soothing sleep listening to Maria.

The first week at Whispering Pines was unbearable. She felt nauseous when food was served on plastic plates. The people who sat around her spit, coughed, and threw food on the floor. Some were drooling. The paper bibs made Constance gag. Constance felt like a homeless woman searching for leftovers in a garbage bin behind a restaurant. Rage gave way to tears. She wept for days. She had no appetite.

When Anthony visited her for the first time, he brought in a small coffeemaker, coffee, cream, and sugar. He had packed Constance's favorite china for her. The deliverymen followed with a small refrigerator. The power of money! The dedication and love Anthony had for Henry and Constance was endearing.

"You could even make tea in this pot," said Anthony, piling bottled water on the shelf. "What else can I do for you, Madam?"

Constance shook her head, "Nothing else, just a hug."

Anthony looked at her. Her sunken eyes—filled to the brim, straining not to spill in front of him, engrossed in fear, confusion, and betrayal—broke his heart. He had been with Henry and Constance for twenty-one years. They were the reason why his only child is a lawyer! He wondered why Constance refused to fight her children like Mr. Cohen wanted her to.

What might be going through her mind? Hurt from treachery, or betrayal, or the shock of it all?

His mind throbbed with irrational thoughts about Constance and he had to leave before he got too emotional. He bowed and left Constance, sulking in distressed thought!

Ebony, Anthony's wife, had wanted to come with him, but she changed her mind.

She said, "I can't visit Constance in there, anyway, not

now." She brushed her tears and walked upstairs to her bedroom. Constance was more of a friend to Ebony than a mistress. Constance wept after Anthony left.

She thought to herself,

What are these tears for? The lost independence of her life? Not being able to drive to the mall, go for a cup of coffee at Starbucks, or just drive around like normal people who did normal things.

Now she is labelled as incapable of taking care of herself. Loss of her independence! Or is loss to be expected? Is someone else telling Constance what to do, without the option of her input or opinion, her new norm? Can she think independently anymore? Is she trapped by the sting of betrayal from her own children rerouting her life to a dead end? She felt as if she was locked in her car, gasping for air as it sank to the bottom of the river after careening off a bridge. No escape!

On a Sunday morning, three weeks after her admission to Whispering Pines, Anthony came to take her to church. He had to convince her to go with him because she was so adamant about not showing her disgraced face at her church, where she had attended service for forty-two years. The thought of the WASPS at the Methodist church with judging eyes eroded her courage every time Anthony offered her reasons why she should be there with her head held high. She had nothing to be ashamed of because of what had happened to her!

Her grandchildren had no clue where their grandma was or what their parents, uncles, and aunts had done. Constance is sure they might have been told that she is away visiting a friend, relative, or someone in Europe and will be away for a while.

Anthony promised her that they would elude the crowd after the service and leave with Martha before the worshippers started filing out. No time for condescension about her children's melancholy descriptions of how their mother has deteriorated!

The residents and employees watched Constance leaving with her chauffeur. She appeared elegant and poised, and most of them wondered if all was well.

Is she going to a funeral?

The employees shared knowing looks. Their eyes exchanged glances that said, *Well, she is really rich! And pompous to be certain.*

Anthony opened the car door and said, "Madam." She got in and the limousine disappeared down the winding driveway of Whispering Pines.

Mr. Hal Blum came to the nurse's station and asked, "Who died"?

Anna Ritter looked at him and shook her head, "No one."

Hal smiled and said, "Good, good."

The relief in Hal's voice was promising enough for Anna. No disruptions now. Hal is okay. His shaking hands rested on the wall and slowly steadied into a flexed metacarpal wall hanging, and he gazed ahead.

Anna knew when his hands started shaking—the first sign of distress and agitation—it took only seconds for him to go into a full-fledged frenzy cocooned in his chaotic reality.

"Hal, they are serving cookies in the day room," Anna said.

Hal smiled and walked in that direction.

Food was his only consolation. He ate anything and everything, wherever he found it. The staff constantly complained about Hal to Mrs. Baker the unit manager, "He is stealing our food."

In her soothing voice, she replied, "Please redirect him. You have to give him reality orientation. He is incapable of discerning the right thing."

The words reality orientation irritated Douglas Chester whenever he heard them. "Really, Ms. Baker, I think we should let them be." Doug knew the consequences of reality orientation.

His definition of reality orientation was, *Hammering nails into the brain and let them scream in agony in a weird euphoria, unidentified and uncertain. Why rake it? Cover it! Let it be.*

If Miss Ruby was around she would add, "They don't know what they are doing."

Douglas Chester remembered the classes on dementia Mrs. Baker sent him to. He was counselled for his indignant definition more than once.

Now he knows better.

He nods when he is in-serviced. He keeps his thoughts to himself and refrains from commenting when his superiors are around.

He told Victoria Stewart and Dolores Cooper in the break room, "I want these humans to be happy. What is wrong in letting their thoughts be reality for themselves? Why wreak havoc?"

"Who knows what their mindset is? Does anyone"? Lisa Mosley asked aloud.

"I am with you," Mirna Childwood walked in and flopped on the chair. "It is killing me, Jesus, it is stressful to all of us, these vexatious moments."

The day's sermon resonated deep inside Constance: Purpose in life! Things happen for a reason, and God's purpose seems unacceptable at the time it happens. But the Almighty has a plan for us all which we might not understand at the time, only to grasp it when least expected.

Constance wondered what her purpose was. She asked God to guide her. Coming out of the church, she saw her children and their families gathered around in conversation. Constance looked at Anthony. He said, "Let's go and have lunch."

Constance nodded, "Just a minute." She walked up to her children, hugged them, and exclaimed, "What a beautiful day." Her grandchildren were in Sunday school. Her kids were taken aback and did not know what to say to their mother.

Finally Sophie said, "Why don't we go inside and get a cup of real coffee before you head back."

Constance replied, "Anthony has a better plan," and she got into her limousine. They lunched at Romano's. Anthony suggested going back to Westchester. Constance replied, "Let me handle everything properly. Whatever I do, everyone will judge me as incoherent and dangerous. We will see."

"Is there anything you need madam?" Constance nodded. "Maybe next time. Not now".

When Anthony dropped her back at Whispering Pines and escorted her to her room, he kissed her in a hurry and left.

Constance joined the residents and visitors wandering around the grounds. She bent down to pick up a withered pine cone. She rolled it in her hand and threw it into the thick woods. She remembered the perfect pine cones she collected from her backyard. Maria passed her. Her shuffling legs kept an unsteady pace ahead of the long, wide steps of her nephew.

The pines whispered sweet nothings to Constance. The hot August sun filled the creases of her face. She smiled as the setting rays of the hot summer sun bowed out in elegance leaving radiant sparkles on her.

Constance thought, *I can smile!* It was the first smile after Henry left her. She looked at Maria and smiled. Maria's nephew nodded and smiled back.

Constance whispered to herself, "I sent a wave of smiles around. These whispering pines and weeping willows acknowledge it. I could begin to love my life here."

The summer sparrows and pigeons fluttered above the weeping willows, chirping in unison and rustling through wavy clouds drifting to the symphony of nature. Entranced by the mesmerizing moment, Constance smiled again. Bathed in the luxury of her surroundings, she inhaled fresh air into her lung's full capacity.

From the clean air outside, Constance went back inside. The dingy, stuffy, gloomy air inside the gray walls of her room suffocated her. The smell of mildew suddenly made her sad. The contentment faded and she stared outside, pining for the life left afar.

CHAPTER 5

Maria Murphy wandered off with her nephew, Father Sean Murphy, a missionary and priest. Fr. Sean was trying to catch up to Maria. When she first saw him, she did not remember him. She stared at him and her complacent smile tortured him. As a missionary, he had travelled through the poorest neighborhoods in the world. Aunt Maria was his idol when he was a kid. At family gatherings commissioned on his behalf when he was in New York, Fr. Sean inhaled all of the wisdom pouring out of Maria. When the day stretched to late night and the wee hours of the morning with all the merriment, he watched Aunt Maria with intensity and yearned for any word of wisdom that spilled out of her. He lashed out at anyone and almost everyone in the family when they referred to her as the "tough spinster" or "Emily Dickinson."

Father Sean looked at Danny and Molly with confusion in his misty blue eyes. Molly caught up to him and said, "Hey, she is okay. There are times when she forgets everything. But, she has asked us about you a million times. Promise! I am a good Catholic girl. I don't lie to priests, even if he is my favorite brother-in-law"!

Father Sean looked at Molly and whispered in a puzzled voice, "How? Why?"

He did not know how to finish his thoughts. He has never choked on his words before, even while in the deep regions of Africa when he was addressing people with sunken eyes. He wrapped them in his eloquent words, driving hope into their hearts, his quick wit giving them strength to strive and live on. When they left, he could see a trace of hope in their tired faces, which gave him reprieve from his own trials and tribulations. Lonely and far away from home, he needed that.

Sean remembered that he did not write to his superiors about his difficult life. He never requested a transfer. He was content and satisfied with his work. He preached the language of the common people and practiced hard work in poverty. In the depths of the dark night filled with the sounds of the jungle, he prayed. He prayed for peace, he prayed for the poor, and he begged God to attend to the basic needs of the people around him.

Father Sean seldom prayed for his family. He was convinced they were not in need of his intercession. When you are on the other side, with people who value one meal as plenty and share what little they have with people around them without being perturbed about their own next meal, he was convinced that his family had too much. No one in the family agreed with him. He was the only priest in the family. They expected him to celebrate baptisms, first communions, confirmations, weddings, and, of course, funerals. Fr. Sean Murphy never obliged these wishes. He could never convince them of his calling. Only Aunt Maria knew who he was. Of course, Danny and Molly adored him.

Sean tried to remember, *Have I attended any family funerals? Any other holy celebrations in the Murphy and O'Connor families?*

None he could remember. He dreaded vacations back in civilization when he was scolded for missing sacred occasions and the indignity of getting a different priest when they had one in the family! The tug of war with family and his calling tormented him when he was huddled in the midst of his family.

If only Aunt Maria was lucid, she would understand him. *Maria Murphy dedicated her life to her mother, family, and students. Is that the life I am leading now? Am I falling into the trap of tunnel vision, ignoring life around me? Is that the way to reach one's goal, where am I? Where is Aunt Maria in it all?* Father Sean wondered.

Weekend visitors were strolling in the backyard with their loved ones. Tired children, dragged in by their mothers, played. Jacob Lawton sat on a wooden bench with his wife, Katherine. Katherine watched the roaring tides looming and receding on the pebbles along the side of the Hudson. Meaningless foams ebbed into dirt and disappeared. Katherine felt overcome with sorrow.

In a way, her life, too, was left in meaningless ebbs and tides, complicated and perplexed by restless nights filled with vivid dreams of unfulfilled leftover life.

In the cryptic arches of her lonely nights, Katherine felt content after washing out her despair in tears that resurfaced uninvited. Katherine looked at Jacob, her Jac. He was staring at a great blue heron perched on the river bank, extending its long neck, eyeing his prey, and fluttering his wide wings as he relocated for a better catch. Katherine smiled.

The pines along the river exuded a sense of belonging. Katherine believed that they whispered to each of the residents, "It is time to belong here." She heard the whisper of the pines in her dreams. Katherine's dreams were shattered by the distrust and fear of leaving Jacob among the gray walls, away from her. Every breath of her thoughts were smothered in hopelessness and unfathomable guilt for placing Jacob at Whispering Pines.

George and Muriel's life fascinated her. As the days passed, George helped to ease her conscious and unconscious fight against all those tangled feelings that left her weary. George talked to her about anything and everything. His words sunk in like the whisper of the pine trees, a soothing lullaby, as gentle as the nightingales on starry nights.

Jacob lost interest in the heron. He turned to Katherine. Katherine's face was relaxed, and a mischievous smile emerged on her lips. She felt Jac staring at her. She leaned over and kissed his right cheek. He did not flutter his eyelids. Katherine realized that Jacob did not feel her. She turned and looked around. She saw Constance under the weeping willow, lost in her own world.

Maria passed Constance, her repetitive movements methodic, but not purposeful. Her actions defined clarity to onlookers, but not to Danny, Molly, and Sean. They sensed the absence of her soul around them. Emily Dickinson stirred in her eroded brain.

"Hope" is the thing with feathers -
That perches in the soul -
And sings the tune without the words -

And never stops - at all -

Aunt Maria whispered. She was lost again for words.

Sean looked at Danny and Molly. They winked at him. Sean, feeling despondent and sad, held his breath, trying to analyze her thought process.

Molly said, "Sean, can you recite the rest of the poem?"

Danny laughed. Katherine shook her head and joined Molly and Danny in a whirlwind of laughter, leaving Sean puzzled.

Constance walked up to them and held Maria's hands. The echo of a horned lark slithered into Maria's soul.

And sweetest- in the Gale –is heard-
And sore must be the storm-
That could abash the little Bird
That kept so many warm-
I've heard it in the chilliest land-
And on the strangest Sea-
Yet- never- in Extremity,
It asked a crumb- of me.

Maria walked along in uncertainty, as vain thoughts circled around her again. Constance sighed.

Father Sean had wanted to say Mass at the Whispering Pines that Sunday, but after spending time with Aunt Maria, he was disturbed by the changes in her and he decided not to. He did not feel up to it. He attended Mass with Danny, Molly, and Maria instead. He held Maria's restless hands. Halfway through the Mass, Maria dozed off into a peaceful nap. Fr. Sean Murphy felt Maria's hands relaxing. He studied her peaceful, relaxed face.

God, why can't she feel like this all the time?

Fr. Sebastian started the sermon. His deep, compassionate voice resonated in the little chapel, "Ask and it shall be given to you, seek and you will find." Sean was stuck with these words, and he did not hear the rest.

He prayed with pain in his heart, "Please God, as your humble servant I have never asked for anything. Take Aunt Maria into your space. Let her roam around in Eden with You. Answer my prayer. I beg you to be merciful to her. Let her not suffer any more in silence. The depth we cannot imagine and feel."

He knelt down. He begged God relentlessly for Mercy. Molly reached over and placed her hand on his shoulders. The poor and the destitute have touched his heart, hurting him, in the past. But Aunt Maria slit it, and he is bleeding out grief and agony now.

What was more hurtful?

Katherine O'Connor Murphy, his mother, with end-stage cancer, lives her life daily, enjoying every moment and aware that life can end any time. She welcomes life and loves her life with a realistic hope of it ending someday, maybe unexpectedly, or expected, as she pictured it: Sean giving her the last rites with family gathered around her to say their goodbyes.

For Aunt Maria, the only humanity left in her is the love of poetry, which she has started to fumble at times. *What is her life like? Is she comfortable? Is she aware of anything in her life?* These dire questions came up in Sean's mind unanswered.

CHAPTER 6

Maria walked along the hallway. She stopped and peeked at Constance. Constance smiled. Maria stayed at the doorway watching Constance. Nina, one of the nursing assistants, came by to escort Maria back to the family room. The employees had to watch Maria to keep her from wandering out of the building. Constance told Nina, "You could leave her with me. I will keep an eye on her." Nina looked at Constance in disbelief. Constance reassured her with a firm nod of her head, then took Maria's hand and walked her into the day room.

Constance had a twinkle in her eyes. She wondered, *What is my purpose? Am I a purpose for this place?*

The elements of tranquility engulfed her distraught self, throbbing with thoughts of her journey toward her true purpose.

Danny and Molly entered the day room and took Maria for a stroll. She whispered,

Does the road wind up-hill all the way?
Yes, to the very end.
Will the day's journey take the whole long day?
From morn to night, my friend.

Molly asked, "Who wrote these lines?" Danny shook his head and looked at Maria, who was staring at the river. Her thoughts had strayed off from Christina Rossetti and wandered to the birds flying above, looking for nests for the night. She wondered and mumbled again, "Is there for the night a resting place"?

Silence thickened among the three. Danny tried to start a conversation about his summer classes, but Maria was deaf and mute. Danny and Molly stood up to walk back with Maria, but she sat still without moving. When Danny helped her to stand, she screamed and became more stubborn. Her screaming annoyed some of the visitors who were strolling and sitting beside of the Hudson, enjoying the evening under the shadows of the pines. Some of them were worried about their own family members imitating or reacting to Maria's behavior, and they walked quickly to get to the safety of their rooms. An elderly lady wheeling her husband gave Danny a fiercely annoyed look. Danny turned red.

Molly said, "Hang on. I will be right back." She ran back to the lobby and took a wheelchair. Ralph, sitting at the security desk, looked at Molly. "What is going on?"

Molly replied, "Aunt Maria is screaming and is refusing to come back."

Ralph called the nurse's station and said, "Molly needs backup. They are near the back."

Everyone at Whispering Pines knew residents and their family members. They watched out for each other. Ralph was alone at the desk, so he couldn't leave. He remembered the day after Maria came to Whispering Pines. The little lady came up to him and asked for a cab. She told him that her car was a 1980 Chevrolet and it was in the shop because the engine needed a tune up. She looked elegant in her pale blue sweater, and her pocketbook hung from her right hand. While waiting for the cab, she talked about the weather and how hard it was to continue as a city school teacher.

When she stepped into the cab she said, "Thank you, young man. Have a good day. I hope I don't end up here like those crazies."

As the cab pulled away Ralph had a feeling of uneasiness, as if something wasn't right. Did I check for an ID bracelet? He had to make sure. His gut feeling bothered him. Yes he was right. Two hours and eleven minutes later, Unit 1 asked him to page a Code E, the elopement code, alerting the whole place to look for Maria. He was concerned about her safety, not his. He had gone against protocol, and the administrator was not on good terms with Ralph. He called Elizabeth Mann, the charge nurse on the unit, and confessed. "I know what happened. I put her in a cab and sent her to 2232 Drake Street."

Elizabeth gasped, "Okay, Ralph, let me call her nephew and see if she is safe." Elizabeth cursed under her breath. Code E's can be as time-consuming as they are nerve-racking. She held her breath and waited for Danny, Maria's nephew, to answer the phone.

He was courteous and said, "I was going to call you. Aunt Maria is home. Her neighbor called me. We lost her so many times in the past. That is the reason we placed her at Whispering Pines."

Elizabeth sighed and said, "Praise be to God. Even the worst of heathens will call His Almighty's name if they work at Whispering Pines," she mumbled under her breath. With relief she said, "Danny, we are so sorry it happened. I am not giving you excuses. She came last night and might have been a new face. So I will immediately send two employees to pick her up and bring her safely back to us."

She deliberately chose words to convince Danny that they were worried about his aunt's safety, and that every measure would be implemented to keep her safe at Whispering Pines.

"I understand. That is why I chose Whispering Pines. Call me anytime. Use my cell. Thank you for calling," Danny said politely.

"Have a good day, sir." Elizabeth hung up, ran to the security desk, and asked the operator to call off the code.

Ralph and Elizabeth went to Maria's apartment and brought her back. Ralph remembered her apartment, neatly lined with mahogany shelves piled with books. Her home looked and smelled like a library. Maria had put up a fight and threatened to call the police because they were intruding. Elizabeth saw agitation creeping across her face as they spoke. She was in situations like this every day. She needed to calm Maria. Elizabeth asked politely, "Can I have a cup of tea?"

Maria obliged. She started the kettle, laid out her china, and waited patiently for the water to boil. Elizabeth talked about the weather and Maria responded, "A hot cup of tea will ward that chill off."

Ralph said, "Darn good tea."

Maria replied, "I don't have any scones or biscuits to go with the tea."

Danny called, and spoke to Maria at length. At the end of the conversation she mumbled, "Alright, alright, bye."

Elizabeth helped Maria put away the dishes. They came out of the apartment in silence and got in the car. During the thirty-minute ride back, she was calm and quiet. Ralph could not read what was in her mind.

When Ralph saw Mirna coming outside with the wheelchair, he snapped back to reality.

"Oh, Ralphie, thank you. Good old Maria, again!" Mirna exclaimed to Ralph. She walked hurriedly down the hill. Danny and Molly looked up at her, worried and exhausted.

Mirna approached Maria and said, "Maria, can we go for dinner? It is six." Maria did not move. Mirna touched her gently. Maria hit her hand. Her face was engraved with knots of anger and despair. Mirna squatted beside her. The disturbed look on Maria's face made her sad.

She said, "Maria, dear, I need your help. That child of mine is failing English. If he can recite a poem by next week, his teacher is willing to pass him. You are my only hope, Maria. I was looking all over for you, and here you are."

Maria stared at Mirna, "How long does he have to memorize it"?

Maria shifted in her wheelchair. Her coiled brain started to unwind. The tight cords relaxed, and she remembered way back when the romantic poets filled her soul and made her giggle.

"What is his assignment about?" Maria asked.

Mirna looked around, hoping for inspiration. *Nephew, dear, help!* her eyes pleaded. Danny understood. Aunt Maria loved Emily Dickinson. The family had nicknamed her Emily Dickinson due to her love of poetry. But she was agitated, and the name could trigger another episode of wrath. It could go either way. What if the name Whitman or Frost sunk in and kindled a lost fire?

Danny whispered to Mirna, "When lilacs last in the dooryard bloomed."

"Oh," Maria looked into the blank space and began to recite,
When lilacs last in the door-yard bloom'd,
And the great star early droop'd in the western
      Sky in the night,
I mourn'd – and yet shall mourn with ever-
      Returning Spring.

The fading sunlight and rising full moon shook hands and lightened the blue gray sky. Maria's voice faded and she mumbled, then let her head rest on the wheelchair. Mirna wheeled her back to the room and put her to bed.

Danny sighed and thanked Mirna, who pulled the floor mattress on the side of the bed for safety just in in case she rolled off the bed and turned the light off. Before she left, she made sure the bed alarm was on. Mirna closed the room gently and moved on to her next assignment. She had to hurry to make up for the time she spent calming Maria.

Danny felt appalled at the whole incident. Each time Molly and he visited, they left with a heavy heart. Chastened and distraught, he squeezed Molly's hands. She nodded back. Aunt Maria used to be vibrant. She took care of her mother and never married. Whenever Danny visited Grandma in her house in Croton, Maria read to him. Everyone used to say he was her favorite. He felt a connection with her that no one understood. He went to church with her and followed her to the library. As he grew older, he called her at least twice a week.

When he had his first job as a teacher at Columbia, Maria sent him a book. At the thought of the book he smiled. Of course she sent him a complete work of Emily Dickinson with gold binding. The note said, "To my math-whiz nephew. When the numbers start to eat your brain, turn to the wise words of the poet who poured out her heart in ecstasy, sorrow, and laughter, and never missed a chance to live. In my opinion, even a dream is worth living for."

Danny had often wondered if Maria gave up her life to take care of her mother.

Did she toughen herself out of a failed love affair? Did she live the lives of her dead poets? Guess no one will ever know.

Maybe after her death he would read the journals that she religiously wrote and left for him, with all her books, for him to have after she passed away. To read them while she was alive would be disrespecting her wishes. His thoughts wandered back to her gift, and he smiled as he drove down the winding driveway

Molly watched her husband's troubled face relax. She knew what he was going through. She reached out and touched his face like Maria did. The first time Danny took Molly to introduce her to Aunt Maria, she had smiled and touched Molly's face. Later, on their way back, Danny explained that was a sign of approval, and now he would take her to meet his parents. Molly admired Aunt Maria. She helped her whenever she was needed. She supported Danny in his need to adjust to his aunt being at Whispering Pines, which was Maria's will. They made sure they visited her, did her laundry, and attended to her personal needs.

Danny turned his face slightly to the right and rubbed his cheek in Molly's hand as he whispered, "Let's stop at Murry's and have a drink."

The day weighed heavily on him, and he needed to unwind before he got home to the kids. Before the road merged into the oncoming traffic, Danny saw an ambulance take a turn right, passing the sign and driving up the winding drive to Whispering Pines. He definitely needed that Henny and coke. Molly nestled her face in his arm and breathed heavily at the reality she never knew, the burden of grief over a human being living a dead life.

God Almighty, have we seen it all? Or is it the beginning of a secret life of an intelligent woman fading away in agony and confusion?

Molly whispered, "Confusion worse confounded." Danny stared at her and burst out laughing.

They were laughing until they parked at Murry's. Neither of them could fathom the reason they were hysterical with laughter. Is it in honor of Aunt Maria's past, a feeble last tribute to her present, or is it a search into her waning, perplexed future?

CHAPTER 7

The spirit of exuberance dwindled in Annabel's heart and rose above to hit the wall of thick fog surrounding her brain. She burst out into scattered pieces underneath a globe of fiery light blinding her, but blasting light enough to keep her vibrant. She screamed in vain. *Where am I?* An increasing waywardness, something not measurable or realistic.

It's not right. I don't know what it is!

Alive! She heard her daughter running around. Fighting to speak and roll over for how long? She felt exhausted. Wishing for rest she closed her eyes, which were already shut tight. Amanda, Annabel's daughter, was trying to pry her eyes open, shouting, "Wake up, Mom! Open your eyes!"

Annabel wanted to say, *I'm okay, just tired, tired. Let me be. Please, can I sleep?* Then she wanted to scream, *I'm scared! The most scared I've felt in all my life. Help me!*

While Annabel tried to float into oblivion while, at the same time, trying to stay awake and talk, feeling tired and wishing to sleep, the next phase of fear made her shudder. She tried to shake it off, but felt helpless. If Maria Murphy had felt this way, she would have said, "Confusion worst confounded." Helplessness wrapped Annabel so tightly that she forgot to breathe. Gasping for air wasn't a priority. *I need to move my fingers, or should I roll over?*

What is happening to me? I can hear everything. Why can't I move or say I am okay. Am I?

Trying to figure it out was exhilarating and exhausting. She heard sirens in the distance.

Is there a fire nearby? Maybe Mrs. Donahue called 911 for her ailing husband! Poor thing! Life is hard enough as it is. Wanting to take care of an ill person at eighty-two is tough.

Annabel heard the front door opening. The sound of boots and the crackle of metal on her wooden floors annoyed her. Muffled voices conversing, mixed with her daughter's words.

What are they talking about? What is happening?

Her brain couldn't give her any answers. She felt helpless and tired. Comprehending waves of flickering attempts to rationalize her chaotic present seemed like a never-ending failed saga of unanswered questions and theories.

Annabel heard every word they said, every question they asked, and every answer they arrived at. Finally she started to shudder.

It is a stroke!

Amanda was asking, "How bad?"

She heard a rough voice replying, "We need to get her to the hospital with a stroke protocol. The earlier we get there, the better the results."

"We will go to St Lawrence. You could follow us, or do you want a ride with us?" Amanda shook her head yes. Or is it no? Amanda was shocked and numb.

What is happening?

Amanda summed up the sense to call Adam, her husband. Alarmed at what he heard, he asked, "What can I do right now?"

"I don't know. The EMTs are telling me that I could go to the hospital. I can't drive."

"Go with them. I will meet you there."

The emergency personnel placed her mother on the stretcher, lifted the stretcher, and rolled it out the door. They lifted her and went down the steps. Amanda walked behind the stretcher. She wanted to hold Annabel tight and say, "Sorry, Mom. I am sorry for everything. What can I do?" Instead she stood quietly, trembling.

One of the men helped her get into the ambulance. He said, "Talk to your mother. She can hear you."

Amanda held Annabel's left hand. Her right hand was limp at her side, with an intravenous running. Amanda looked at the dripping fluid and the fierceness of the fluids pumping sustenance into her mother. Her eyes were closed, and she had an oxygen mask over her face.

The sirens blasted the quiet neighborhood. Annabel realized that she had never had such fear consume her, ever in her life. A helpless series of events that she had no control over! Her eyes gripped shut, her lips twitched, and her half-open mouth left her choking and gasping for air. Amanda said, "Look, she is gasping, dying. Oh my God"!

The paramedic suctioned her mouth open and propped up her head. Annabel wanted to say, *Amanda, dear, I am okay.*

But she can't say it. She couldn't say anything. The mother–daughter fights, the arguments, and the intimate details of their lives, all shattered in one moment. Annabel had the words to express her feelings, but was unable to do so!

The quiet of the surroundings ceased as they reached the hospital. Movements, whispers, loud commands, bright lights, and Amanda's unexpressed tears, they all seemed to wane and wax in and out of Annabel.

The last thing she remembered was men and women stripping off her clothing and hooking her to monitors, bright lights blinding her, machines beeping in different tones, loud noises, louder than at home and, after being stuck in a cave, she totally lost it and slept with exhaustion. Maybe the medications anesthetized her to peaceful frontiers. The longing to fight it all or give up left her mind reeling. And then came peace, and she was in a deep sleep.

When she woke up in a strange room with unfamiliar sounds and whispers of machines, her fear came back. Annabel tried to call out for help. Her throat felt closed up. Her mouth was dry. She tried to wet her chapped lips, and her tongue slid to the left side.

What is happening to me?

Something weird was crawling quietly inside, but she was unable to discern and dissect the feeling. Sweat sprouted from every pore. Cold hands swept over her, and she lost track of everything.

Amanda paced restlessly for hours that seemed like days and nights without end. She watched her mother being wheeled off to the CT scan and back, neurologists and intensivists nodding their heads, scanning computers and consulting. She watched a blond nurse chewing her gum vigorously while trying to add a new line to hang multiple bags of fluids. Amanda could not understand what was what. It was the first time she was in dread of the distress and uncertainty of the unknown.

What is happening to Mom?

Mother was the only family left in the world for her. She had no memory of her father. With no brothers or sisters, she was left with her mother. They fought with each other every day. They were as tight as could be. Amanda started to cry.

Amanda felt a pair of hands holding, supporting, and embracing her. It was a woman in blue scrubs. She handed her a cup of coffee. Actions that spoke a thousand words! Amanda was happy that the blue-dressed woman did not speak to her. She was in no mood to answer questions. Her mind was blank. She wished she had a sibling to help carry the burden of this moment with her.

Waiting for answers, Amanda held her warm coffee cup tightly, but she forgot to sip it. The heat made her hands red and fiery. She sat still, refusing to breathe as if that would steer her mom toward a worse condition.

She is so fragile. She is alone and scared. Is she cold or warm? Amanda was on the verge of a panic attack when Adam walked in. He held her trembling and cold body tightly in his arms.

"I don't know what is going on," Amanda said.

"I will find out. Relax. Let's be strong for Mom" he whispered in her ear. Adam rubbed her shoulders and neck. He felt the roaring tension inside her as her muscles turned tight. He eased her to the chair and said, "I will be right back." He walked toward the double door separating them from the patients inside. He approached the nurse at the desk and said, "I am Annabel Strand's son."

Before he finished what he intended to say, the nurse motioned him to follow her. He entered a room separated by a thick curtain. Annabel lay still, curling wires spread all over her skin. The beeps and the alarms of the machines scared Adam. A nurse was busy adjusting them and talking to Annabel as she worked on her.

"Maryann, this is Adam, Annabel's son." Adam had introduced himself as her son because he was not sure if they would give him any information if he told them he was her son-in-law.

The nurse turned around and her ID bore the name Maryann Hirsch. She stretched out her hand and said, "Maryann. Adam, come closer." She pulled out a stool and asked him to sit down.

"Hold her hands or touch her and talk to her. Annabel can hear you." She touched his shoulders, and Adam felt her compassion and concern. He squeezed her hand and said, "Thank you."

Adam was scared to touch Annabel. He looked at Maryann, who nodded. "It's okay."

Annabel felt Adam touching her. She felt his warmth, concern, and fear. She wanted to say, *I am okay. How is Amanda? Be with her. I will be fine.* Through her fear, she tried to say it. She couldn't.

As Annabel lay limp, Adam went out to speak with the doctor. The neurologist stepped outside with him. He sat down opposite Amanda, with Adam next to her.

The start of a different life for all of us

Adam whispered in his mind, and he knew the path ahead would be filled with thorns and stones. He sighed and held his wife.

The path ended at Whispering Pines. Amanda looked into the place after the case manager at the hospital provided the names of neighboring rehabilitation centers that could accept Annabel and attend to her present needs.

What are her needs? Amanda wondered, but dared not ask.

She nodded her head. As she listened, her eyes were overflowing.

The case manager handed her a tissue and shook her head, staying quiet for a minute to give Amanda time to digest the information. Amanda left the room with a brochure for Whispering Pines. She had invited her pastor, Jeremiah, and his wife, Elina, for dinner. The family needed guidance and, of course, divine intervention. Amanda and Adam's children—Ted, Michael, and Julianne—were very upset about Grandma. The Grandma they knew was vibrant and lively, and she had taken care of them from the time they were born. Sunday dinner at Grandma's was very special for them.

When Adam and Amanda went on vacation, or out to dinner, or attended parties, the kids were happy to be with Grandma. Ted, eighteen, was the first grandchild of the family. Annabel was in seventh heaven when he was born. She spoiled him whenever she had a chance. Even at eighteen, when Adam and Amanda had difficulty getting through to Adam, Annabel was their saving grace.

Often, Amanda heard him mumbling, "Why can't you be like Grandma?"

"I heard that. I grew up with her. I know she wasn't that great to me." Whenever Annabel heard that, she laughed and said, "Well, I knew you were great."

Their grandma now looks at them and with eyes full of fear and confusion, and bangs her hand on the table. All she says is, "Okay, okay!"

The family stood, wondering.

Amanda looked outside. The scorching heat of summer rippled off the pavement. She saw shadows and figures in the middle of golden silhouettes. She whispered, "My mom's golden years! Scattered in shadows and figures she cannot express."

She did not try to hide her tears. Pastor Jeremiah stood up and extended his hands. Elina stood on her other side and they prayed for peace, fortitude, and wisdom in their time of need. He added, "May the Lord be with this family, connecting them in one spirit. May their lives be filled with gratitude for the good moments and understanding for moments that are not comprehensible to human intelligence."

A reverence filled the room. They sat silently and ate. Even the kids made sure they did not make any noise with their cutlery.

The kids were surprised there was homemade dessert. Amanda had made her mother's apple pie. She wanted the kids to savor Grandma, and did not want them to feel that all is lost and there is no turning back.

There is hope.

She smiled as she cut the pie and served it first to Ted, Michael, and Julianne, surprising them. The adults nodded their heads in agreement.

CHAPTER 8

Katherine sat on the wooden lounge chair and passed a cup of café latte, Jacob's favorite. He stared at the coffee cup. He has forgotten to bring it to his lips and drink.

Katherine leaned over and helped him take the first sip. His eyelids fluttered, and Katherine knew he recognized the taste, maybe the smell. Somehow, she knew he was enjoying it. How can she know? He is her Jacob, and she knows it as only she can know.

Katherine's blue eyes turned misty. Jacob looked up at her as he finished with his coffee.

He reached out with his right hand and wiped her tears. Then he shook his head as if telling Katherine, "Don't cry. I am here." His face was blank. He stared as if he was blind and oblivious to touching Katherine's flesh. She did not see the fluttering lashes.

Annabel was pounding on the glass door saying, "Okay, okay."

Katherine looked around. Annabel was alone. She might have wandered outside and did not know how to open the sliding glass doors to get back inside.

Annabel paced restlessly and pounded on the door again. Katherine got up from the wooden chair, walked up to Annabel, and touched her hands gently. Annabel looked at Katherine with confusion and fear nestled in her eyes.

"It's okay. I will help you," Katherine said.

"Okay, okay," Annabel flapped her hands together and moved away from Katherine. She did not like to be touched, but she had no way of communicating that.

Katherine looked inside and spotted Dolores Cooper who

came outside to help Annabel.

As Katherine sat back down next to Jacob, who was already napping, she returned to her thoughts about her husband.

What has my life attained by focusing on doing everything right to live a full life? I know what to say inside. But I can't! I am trying and trying, and then I get frustrated and agitated. If I get agitated, I get up and run across the hall to nowhere and hit my head. My mind is willing, but my body refuses to come with me and I can't control my limbs to take me where I want to go.

Jacob was trying to strategize his next move, something he could do without causing a calamity.

The last time Jacob Lawton tried to walk out of his room to get a breath of fresh air when he was feeling suffocated, he collapsed in front of the nurse's station around one in the morning. The hustle and bustle of running nurses, phone calls, and the sirens of the ambulance were the last thing he remembered. He woke up some time later attached to multiple tubes, including one down his throat. He struggled hard to pull up off the bed, but his hands were tied and the nurse sedated him.

Every day after coming to Whispering Pines he fought—to walk, to talk, to take a stroll outside for fresh air, or even to take a bath. He loved his baths at bedtime. After a stressful day at Lawton Enterprises, he came home to Katherine and his two sons. They led a normal family life. They watched their children doing their homework and cooked supper together.

When it was time for bed, he ran his bath. He regularly bought relaxing soaks for his bath. He listened to calming music while he was in the tub, and after thirty minutes he was ready for bed. When in the company of his golf buddies, he boasted about his good night's sleep, even during tax season. At fifty-three, he had never taken any sleeping pills or antidepressants.

Katherine was the first to notice her husband forgetting small things around the house. She believed he was busy and forgot little things. One day she waited at the restaurant to meet him for dinner, but he never showed up. She was unable to locate him. When she finally located him on his cell phone, he was in an emergency room waiting to be tended to for a laceration on his forehead. He said he hit his head on a pole while trying to get into a cab to go to Third Street to meet his mother.

His mother! Third Street! Katherine was appalled. *What is he talking about? Maybe he has a concussion.*

Katherine hurried to the ER and found Jacob in utter confusion. He was not able to tell the staff any pertinent information. He looked puzzled, confused, and scared, as if he was out of his comfort zone. When he saw Katherine, his face lit up. Her presence, so familiar to him, brought him back to reality. The doctor in the ER stitched the gushing laceration on his forehead, wrote a prescription for pain medicine, and advised him to stay home for two days. The doctor assured them the CT scan was fine and said he needed rest.

Katherine was curious to know why he was so confused when she came in, but the physician replied, "It's normal after you have a head injury. He is oriented now. If anything changes, please contact your primary care physician for follow up." He shook her hand and walked away in a hurry.

Katherine started to observe Jacob, and saw that he was unable to communicate with her at times. He waved his right hand a lot while talking to her. He said, "Anyhow," repeatedly. Katherine was struck with a bigger picture, the one that she had to live with for the rest of her life. He was discharged with a diagnosis of stress-related alteration in mental status.

"With rest, he will be fine," the nurse who discharged him from the ER reinforced. Jacob shook his head for everything the discharge nurse was going over.

Tax season dragged him into its monstrous routine. Katherine noticed a black mark on his right elbow, and he said he might have hit his arm, but did not remember doing it. Katherine coaxed him to see a neurologist.

"I will, as soon as the tax season is over." Scratching his head, he asked, "When is tax season over"?

"What"? Katherine was shocked. "Honey, what is going on?" She was scared

For months, she had noticed that he was forgetful at times, but occasionally had progressed to more often. He started to lash out at Katherine and the kids without any provocation. That was unusual. One day, he ended up in an emergency room without knowing what he was doing, where he was going, or who to call!

Jacob Lawton, the math wizard, attributed his forgetfulness and temper to stress and long hours. His body was often tired. Katherine saw the love of her life becoming wildly different as days passed. Only a person who was close to him could see the change in him.

Katherine felt uneasy about the whole situation.

Something is not right. She said it over and over again to herself. *I need to get to the bottom of it.*

Katherine made up her mind to persuade Jacob to get medical attention. She could not shrug away the uneasy feeling that was brewing in the pit of her stomach.

As the days passed, his memory became more fogged. He remembered her cell number when he ended up in the ER. It was her number that he remembered! She felt elated. Even in the worst of situations, she was near and dear to him. This was a stray of relief for Katherine.

Then she went right back to that queasiness of impending doom.

What could be wrong? Is it stress? Or am I paranoid?

Katherine couldn't reach a conclusion.

She made an appointment with a neurologist for April 16th, and Jacob threw a storm of accusations at her. She was bewildered at his discombobulated behavior. She always made his medical appointments. *What is this anger about?*

Who am I to him? Am I an outcast, and there's someone new? Katherine asked herself.

It could be more, her reason, intuition, and love whispered to her.

What is it? I don't know. What should I do?

Jacob came around, hugged her, and said, "I don't know

what is happening to me."

Katherine had no answer. They hugged as if they were in a chasm together, unable to pull out of what was going on in their lives.

She said, "Honey, we are fine. Relax. I am right here."

She felt at peace for the moment. It lasted until Seth Hamilton, his co-worker, called and asked, "Is Jacob okay? Is he stressed?"

"Why? Is everything okay?" Katherine replied.

"I don't know, Kate. Something is wrong. Well, let's see. Please don't worry." He hung up without much more discussion. His tone made her perplexed. It was the mystifying tone, the one she hated.

The verdict when he had his appointment on April 16th shattered their perfect life.

"Early onset dementia."

From then on, Jacob Lawton regressed as quickly as the blink of an eye, and he ended up at Whispering Pines.

In physical therapy, Katherine noticed Annabel. All she said was "Okay."

Amanda told her, "My mother had a stroke."

They exchanged pleasantries. Sometimes George joined in their conversations. They supported each other.

They are connecting already! Women and their cosmic sympathetic intuitions and belief in their Karma and what not? Maybe a cosmic balance to their existence!

Jacob did not understand Maria, Constance, or any of the other residents. Out of courtesy and habit, he nodded his head to acknowledge them. Katherine stopped to have conversations with residents and families. They have evolved into her life, uninvited and unknowingly.

Now she has the confidence to hug Maria or start a conversation with Constance or George. At times, she even walks up to the nurse's station and makes a gesture to draw the nurses' attention to a wetter who needs to be changed, an eloper who needs to be redirected, or even to diffuse some turmoil between two residents.

Jacob had been a math whiz. He was unable to speak and identify with any of them!

What is Annabel Strand crying about? Why does she try to speak and finally shakes her head violently and start hitting it on the wall behind her?

Occasionally, he shared a baked goodie Amanda passed around while he sat with Katherine. Although he never understood what they were whispering and agreeing and disagreeing on, he sat quietly munching the sweet treat and sipping coffee.

Life in its uncalculated wisdom let loose something that everyone else devoured as right and perfect, but that he thought of as insane.

To an onlooker, from the outside every trundled sequence is insane and out of context.

Minnie Blackwood moved around, humming. She did not look around, nor did she acknowledge anyone. She just kept walking. Occasionally, she turned and looked back. Katherine sighed. She wanted to alert a staff member that Minnie was alone outside, but she felt too lazy to get up. She was relieved when she saw Dolores escorting Minnie inside.

One day, Katherine got a call saying Jacob was being rushed to the emergency room at St Mary's. The nurse who called from Whispering Pines took a deep breath and said, "Mrs. Lawton."

It took Katherine minutes to regain her composure and say, "Yes?"

"Mr. Lawton had a fall. We are not sure what happened. He was found unresponsive on rounds, and he is on his way to the hospital. I'm sorry to bother you at this time."

Katherine pictured Jacob in an ambulance heading to St Lawrence, scared and unable to say, "Stop! Let me out." His whole life's work dedicated to numbers, scores, and savings, that unknowingly led him now to a life of bondage and torture that wouldn't compute for him. He spent his life reducing financial uncertainty for his clients. He made sure their futures were safe and secure.

Where is safety when the mind and body feels scared and secluded? What has life become for the brainiac everyone admired.

Jacob lost all of it in the days he spent at Whispering Pines. Katherine waited for Jacob to get settled at the hospital.

Katherine poured herself a drink. She stared at the phone and waited and waited. She hoped it rang and gave her good news. For eleven months she never received good news. She would have been happy with the news that she could relax and Jacob was going back to Whispering Pines. Finally she dialed the hospital and the young lady who answered the phone told her, "Ma'am, he is in triage."

"Thank you, I am coming. I will be there in fifteen minutes," Katherine replied.

"Please stay home. I will call you as soon as he is settled. They will be busy running tests, and you will have to wait before you see him. I promise, I will call you and then you can come and stay with him. Give me your number."

Katherine provided her home and cell numbers, just in case.

She sipped her drink, drew a blanket over her, and leaned back on the couch. She balanced her glass in her right hand and pressed her left hand to her pulsing temple. The night dragged by.

The warmth and stillness of comfort was lost on Jacob.

He wanted to scream and say, *Let me out!*

Wrapped in warm blankets, unable to move or talk, he struggled to make some noise, which was lost in his throat somewhere.

"I am walking a path without regrets,
Only a faint smile!
I never knew I could do this –
Scattered molecules working hard to close out
And pinpoint a thought.
It appears impossible at times
No, all the time!
They whirl in me to come out.
They can't.

There are times when they flash a graceful glimpse of light
A fraction of a second
They stick on hard
And gone astray
Without coming up
I can't say it!
I know it! I know it!
What use is, knowing if I don't share it?"

The thundering noise of the MRI machine dragged on, and Jacob tried to stay awake and count. His favorite numbers flowed easily, and he was relieved that he was awake and alive. He breathed and played with numbers, and it made him happy. His twitching muscles and his constrained effort to scream and struggle started to fade when he concentrated on numbers. He sighed and breathed evenly. The alarming distress floated away. He felt at ease. He felt alright.

He did hear the staff shout, "Come on, Code Blue, start CPR!"

Maybe God the father looked down from the Garden of Eden and grabbed up the best flower he saw that day on earth for His garden. Always the best for Him. Maybe life was kind and had him in real oblivion where he felt no suffering.

The mysteries of life unraveled in front of all the nurses and doctors pumping and laboring to bring Jacob back to their custody.

It took thirty minutes for them to turn back and say, "Time of death, two thirteen a.m."

Katherine waited. She felt calm and at ease and she sensed Jacob with her. *This feeling is not good.* Katherine panicked.

The boys came running down the stairs and said, "Where is Dad? We thought he was here!"

CHAPTER 9

Guiseppina was having the worst dream she had ever had. She screamed at the top of her voice, "Luigi, help me! The children are killing me!" The shadows that attacked her were vague, but with enough distinct concrete concepts to fill her mind with fear. The fear she fills herself which comes from abstract images haunting and haunting until they explode and Guiseppina rides as if she is on ecstasy. It is hard to control her when she gets into these moods.

Ruby was finishing her rounds and starting to document, when she heard the scream from Guiseppina's room. She mumbled, "Sweet Jesus, she is going to wake all of them." Her heavy legs waddled as fast as she could. Celine Matthews, the night nurse, ran ahead of Ruby. Guiseppina was sitting on her bed trying to take the side rails down. When she failed, she attempted to climb over the side rails. The bed alarm went off. The shrieking noise of the alarm made her more agitated. The lights were turned on in the room.

Ruby said, "Thank God she did not fall. That crazy daughter will create a mayhem. Thank you Jesus."

Celine had also come running. Letting out a sigh of relief she said, "She didn't fall. Let's go. We should put her back to bed." Carefully, they removed Guiseppina's legs from between the side rails. It took three of them to put her back to bed. Guiseppina kept fighting and cursing. She was sweating.

"Can we give her something to relax her?" Ruby looked at Celine.

"No, we can't. She had her medications at bedtime. You will have to sit with her until she calms down. I don't want any falls on my watch."

Ruby sat with Guiseppina. She tried to talk to her and position her. Nothing was working. Finally, Ruby put Guiseppina in a wheelchair and wheeled her to the nurse's station. Celine pulled out a reclining chair and helped Guiseppina transfer from the wheelchair. She fought like a scared cat, kicking and scratching them and cursing in English and Italian. Guiseppina continued her angry tirade.

"God help us. It will be a wild and long night." Ruby looked at her co-workers.

"Please do something," Ruby said.

It was directed at Celine. She went inside the medication room and came out with a glass of cranberry juice. "Here, dear, please take a sip. It's your favorite, cranberry juice. You might be really thirsty." Celine motioned the others to back off. She pulled a chair up and started talking to Guiseppina.

"Are you cold"? Guiseppina stared at her. "Can I cover you with a blanket?" She had kicked her blanket off her body. Celine Matthews sat with her until Guiseppina turned to her. Celine placed the straw in her lips and she started to drink. Halfway done, she pushed the cup away and began wiggling, trying without success to get out of the chair. Celine waited patiently until Ruby came back and motioned her to get up.

Ruby sat next to Guiseppina and started singing "Ave Maria." Guiseppina listened. Ruby gave her some cookies that she had brought out of Guiseppina's room. The family always kept an ample supply of cookies and pastries for her. Ruby laid out the juice and cookies in front of her and encouraged her to eat. She tasted the cookie and offered to share with Ruby. Ruby shook her head and declined politely. Ruby kept singing in her angelic voice. Guiseppina ate her cookies, then Ruby cleaned her up and asked if she wanted to go to the ladies room. Guiseppina did not answer. Ruby and Veronica checked to make sure she was not wet. They reclined her and positioned her comfortably. Guiseppina started singing,

Ave Maria, gratia plena

Maria, gratia plena
Maria, gratia plena
Ave, Ave dominus

Guiseppina went on singing the same lines and finally closed her eyes. Her rhythmic breathing and relaxed hands let the staff be sure she was sleeping. "Two hours, and that nasty daughter has no clue. My, my, what a life," Ruby exclaimed.

Celine said, "Now you are talking like Guiseppina." They laughed.

Guiseppina floated into the wings of her dreams. She dreamed about her three children. She saw Ariana her daughter running towards mother in a hurry

Ariana's clicking heels scared her. The tail end of the dream was Ariana yelling at Luigi and Bill while their spouses looked blankly at her. Ariana had decided to remodel their old house and place Guiseppina in a safe place. Guiseppina was losing her memory, and her life would be in danger living with Luigi and his wife because her daughter found out that her mother had dementia. Her daughter felt that she has to be placed somewhere appropriate for her mental status. Life has taken a worse turn for Guiseppina. Luigi and his wife were willing to take care of Mamma at home. But the educated Ariana, the only daughter, who is married to a Wall Street guy with money, did not agree. Mother was safe at a place like Whispering Pines. She knew better!

Guiseppina hated her daughter anyway! She never did anything right. Luigi and Bill were the best. That made Ariana crazy, to the extent of having fights at holidays and family gatherings.

"Well, my boys were the best and if I did not give birth to a daughter my life would have been so different," Guiseppina shared with the staff.

The thought made Guiseppina mad, to the extent that she cursed and screamed. Nobody knew what went through her mind.

Ariana was concerned about her mother when she noticed bruises on her body. Her nurse mode kicked in. She started to make surprise visits and call on Guiseppina unannounced. Many a time she saw Guiseppina immersed in deep thoughts, and she got agitated when she could not answer simple questions. The aversion on her face frightened Ariana. She meant well when she started talking to her brothers about her suspicions. She even contacted Dr. Morton and was furious at his lecture on privacy and his suggestion to, "Talk to your mother about your concerns." Ariana was greatly worried about her mother's safety.

Appalled and confused by the turn of events, Ariana was frightened beyond reason. Slowly, the grasp of changes in her mother shuddered into a cold spasm of evil reality. Guiseppina was slowly fading into another world, a world no one else was privy to. Dealing with the family dynamics and cultivating a realistic goal was beyond her domain. Somehow she had to convince Bill, Luigi, and their wives, which was an incomprehensible task. Ariana would rather move to the West Coast and hide than plunge into the middle of reality.

Guiseppina was napping in her recliner. She dreamed about watching the boys and their father play in the pool. Her husband had built the pool for the boys one summer. Life has taken them on many routes filled with uphills and downhills, but they always survived and kept going forward. This is the last stop. Staring into the distance, Guiseppina was unaware of any of it. She did not even think of asking, *Why am I here?* or *Is this right for me?*

CHAPTER 10

The recreation room smelled of fresh coffee. The music therapist was playing her guitar and singing, "Take me out to the ball game." She was walking around and encouraging the residents to participate. Charles, the nursing assistant, was busy passing out refreshments.

Ruth Fisher was rocking back and forth. She shouted, "Don't you know anything else. A stupid ball game! Stupid bitch, what nonsense is this?"

Charles approached Ruth and gave her chocolate pudding. He helped her to peel the cover off and discard it. The plastic spoon was in her left hand, and Charles fed her the first spoon of pudding. This was a cue for Ruth to taste the chocolate pudding and continue to eat. Charles straightened the bib.

"Good old Charles to the rescue," George and Liz acknowledged him.

"Coffee, tea, or juice," he mumbled in front of the residents.

Constance mused, "He must be talking with respect. It appears like a whisper." The cookie tray followed the pudding and apple sauce. George helped Charles wake people up, open their juice, and added milk or sugar to coffee for people who needed it. Finally, George settled down next to Muriel with a cup of coffee and a chocolate pudding. He carefully started feeding Muriel with a loving smile. He sang along with the music therapist, sipping his coffee, feeding Muriel, and encouraging others to sing.

Constance eyeballed the room. In her world, refreshments were elegant with tea and tea sandwiches, bite-size pieces of cake, and fluffy pastries served on classic china with silverware and cloth napkins. She thought about her favorite Royal Albert Old

Country Roses Pink Vintage collections, the fun teatimes with Sophia. The memories of teatime with her friends brought a nauseating wave of nostalgia and another reminder of the loss of her independence. When Charles came to her, she took a paper cup, poured herself tea, and thanked him.

Constance said to herself, *Now I am used to all of these paper cups and the filthy smell surrounding me. But I feel a sense of peace and warmth. This is the first time after my husband died that I am accepting my present, this moment is a real one."*

Nadia's daughter, Ellen Monroe, walked in with an air of arrogance. She went straight to her mother, who was cooped up on the sofa eating her cookie and sipping pale coffee. Charles concocted Nadia's coffee with lot of milk and no sugar, the way she liked it. She had spilled coffee on her yellow blouse, which had multiple coffee stains. She had taken off the paper bib and thrown it on the floor. Charles concentrated on mixing coffee for Maria. He wanted to avoid Ellen because he knew there was going to be a problem from the look on her face. Elizabeth Mann gave Annabel her medication mixed into her chocolate pudding and, when she was done, quietly left the room to avoid confrontation with Ellen Monroe.

The music therapist was winding down. She placed her guitar on the table and said, "Thank you, everybody. Good job. See you all tomorrow."

Ellen took the coffee cup out of Nadia's hand. The cookie crumbs were all over the floor, and on Nadia's clothes and face. Ellen turned around and demanded of Charles, "Who is in charge?"

"Mom, please let go of that nasty cup." Ellen was boiling with emotions. Constance tried to figure it out.

Is it fear or grief or both, ready to burst and masking it all with an act of disgust and anger? Does she feel anything at all? Or is she numb from the pressure of it all? How can she look at her once-elegant mother and see her wasted to no recognition?

When Ellen passed Constance, she nodded and turned her head to Charles who was trying to wipe Nadia's face and hands with a wet cloth. Ellen looked at her mother and stared at the coffee stain on her yellow blouse. She reverted to a fit of rage and stopped Charles, "I need the person in charge. The money I pay to this place! Look at my mother. This does not look like my mother. I cannot believe it. God forbid, if she had no one."

When she knew she was getting some much-needed attention from the small gathering in the room, she shook her head in disgust. George read her expression of disgust as *I don't know how to look at my mother, who has turned into a stranger to herself and to me.*

Nadia was not aware of anything going on around her. She smiled and mumbled. The elegant mother Ellen was used to looked distracted, filthy, and remote. Above all, she did not recognize Ellen or, if she did, she did not know how to express that recognition.

Mrs. Baker waved to Ellen and motioned her to come outside. Mrs. Baker was the nursing care manager for the unit. Her calm face and deep, compassionate eyes pierced through the deep layers of Ellen's paralyzed feelings. She gently motioned Ellen to her room. The walls of her room had witnessed many a family member when they voiced their concerns and convictions of right and wrong.

Dolores wheeled Nadia to her room to clean and change her. Maria was walking in the hallway, squabbling, unaware of Dolores and Nadia passing her.

"I grow old—I grow old—
I shall wear the bottoms of my trousers rolled.
And what—."

Maria panicked. *What did Elliott say after that?*

George wheeled Muriel around and wondered, *Can she remember the end or the beginning?* He looked down at Muriel, "*Can she ever remember me? Is oblivion a bliss or a curse?*

Pacing faster and faster in exhilarating sacrilege, Maria composed her mini poem.

Distress is upon me,
Nowhere to turn, run and hide

Alone and forgetful
I don't remember! How could I not?
The chill of fear surrounds me.
Where am I?
Was I always wrong?
Is anyone around to stand up and pull me up from the girth?
The evolving door is shutting, squeezing me
Come around and hold me
Pull me up and hold me
A breath of peace
Erase my panic
Let me stop running
I am tired.
Can I rest!
Can I?
 No one is around to say
"Yes,
Yes, you are safe!"

Maria leaned against the armoire in the recreation room. Her face was pale and panicked. She looked exhausted. Constance got Charles to get one of the nurses. Liz and Anna walked in with the wheelchair. Maria became extremely difficult when she worked herself into a manic state.

Liz was quick to place the wheelchair behind her and said, "Maria, can I take you to get a cup of tea?" Her voice was calm and gentle, and she was careful not to add to Maria's panicked state.

Constance smiled to herself. *They know each of their residents, and they know what to tell them.* She has learned to admire the nursing staff each day. The way they diffuse mood swings and care for the lost minds and bodies with compassion and empathy. They take their jobs to their hearts.

Maria held tight to the end of the armoire. Anna anticipated some difficulty with moving Maria safely from the room. She said, "Charles, please move the residents to the solarium."

George volunteered to help. Liz and Anna stayed with Maria. They did not speak or touch Maria. Mirna came in and started moving residents, saying, "Let's watch a movie in the solarium."

"Is it full moon?" Lisa Mosley said aloud as she wheeled

Albert Crowley, who smiled, an automatic reflex to his favorite care takers voice. Constance watched all of them at the same time. *If Maria starts screaming it will agitate a majority of them.* Guiseppina looked puzzled. One false move, and the room would turn into pandemonium.

Ellen was coming out of Mrs. Baker's office and appeared much calmer, although her mascara was mushy. She saw her mother wearing a blouse with no coffee stain. She sighed. Nadia had hit her on the head with a spoon for spilling coffee on her shirt when she was a little girl, and now her mother is herself disheveled and unaware of it. The appropriate, elegant lady has a filthy mouth now.

Where did it come from? Was she suppressing her bad self all these years? Is that why she has dementia and unleashes her lousy attitude freely, the opposite of what she strived to instill in me by force and love? Ellen wondered to herself.

Ellen smiled, unaware of her own feelings. Mrs. Baker listened, nodded, and touched her with gentle manicured fingers. She felt her mother reaching out to her saying "Let go, it is okay. This is my life now." *Is it the truth?* She looked around and watched the family members conversing with each other and the residents. They even laughed with the employees. There were hugs and "Thank yous" and "See you soons."

Can I blend in? What other choice do I have? Ellen wished for the gift of reality. *Maybe, some day she could bring her son and daughters to visit Grandma.* Ellen felt happy that she had three kids. They won't be lonely like her. As the only child, making decisions for her mother was very tiresome. The intensity of it all made her mad, angry at everyone and anyone she could take it out on. To choose correctly and the process of it all made her tired. Her nerves ran wild. She knew that if she continued like this she herself would be locked up in an asylum soon. Maybe a stroke or her tired heart will stop beating. Whatever it is, it's imminent.

Ellen was thankful that she had run into Mrs. Baker. She listened and listened. She nodded her head in acknowledgement when needed. Mrs. Baker handed her tissues when she needed them. Ellen's concerns about her mother vanished, and Ellen stopped. Puzzled and guilty, she looked at Mrs. Baker. She saw empathy and honesty looking back at her.

"I cannot even imagine what you are going through right now." Mrs. Baker held Ellen's hands.

Ellen looked at Mrs. Baker's hands. Soft and well-manicured fingers, jeweled with an expensive rock. The gentle touch was soothing. Ellen felt embarrassed.

Oh my God, why am I judging her hand and her ring?

Mrs. Baker sensed her feelings and replied, "It's Okay. I get it a lot and I love it."

Ellen sighed.

Mrs. Baker said, "I am sorry to tell you that what you are seeing in your mom is real. There is no coming back. But this is not the end of it. As days go by, it will get easier. Start with talking to the other family members."

Mrs. Baker pulled out a schedule book and handed it to Ellen. "Programs and support services we have here for families. Some of them are with your mom, some with other families, and we are here if you need to talk. Just look at them when you have time." She added, "Mostly, tea and talk, and when it all ends you breathe much better."

Mrs. Baker winked her right eye, "You will feel near normal in the group."

What is normal? Nothing will ever feel normal! Is near normal the new normal for me? Ellen nodded.

Mrs. Baker always knew the right thing to say. Above all she knew when to stop. Brevity is well appreciated, especially when it gets the point across smoothly, like a breeze, to soothe bewildered psyche.

Ellen exhaled hard as she stepped out of the office to the corridor leading to the rec room. She wiped tears of distress and hopelessness from her face. She had learned to pile tissues in her pocket book—*Hey, a new norm!*—any time she visited Mom.

Ellen breathed hard. *Did I ever listen to Mother? What a ridiculous question!*

I am glad Mother said I was a lot like her before her oblivion! A safe haven! Well, I am always confused and short of being decisive. Wishing for a sibling for the first time. I could blame him or her and my mother. Daddy was out of the question. I never knew him. He died in the war. What a fucking honorable man!"

Ellen felt her mother's core. *How could she have been sane enough to raise me? Well, she is out of it now, and in a better place than when she was with me.*

Guilt started to creep back in after it had evaporated in Mrs. Baker's room. *Am I in all ways my mother's daughter? Every second of her life was for me. I always hated my life growing up and shamed her whenever I could! I withered her inner soul and acted as her worst nemesis.*

The group it is. Or else I am done too. With no siblings, a family of my own except her- The one I tormented all her life for her unselfish dedication to me.

Ellen sat on the floor, hunched over. *How long?* No clue. She felt the warm hands of Amanda.

The next thing she knew was hearing herself say, "I miss her and I miss him. Why"? She was in George's sturdy hands.

George caressed her like she was his own firstborn, pining for her mother.

Ellen watched the staff moving residents around Maria in her manic state and the protective staff around her. She walked up toward Constance and said, "Hello."

Constance held her hand and said, "Nice to meet you. Please sit down."

Constance asked Charles if she could have a cup of coffee. He came with the coffee cart.

"Black, light, or straight up?" he laughed, and Ellen knew it was genuine. He handed her the warm cup.

"Black with two sugars."

"We don't allow residents to pour coffee. You can have a cup anytime you feel like having a cup of java. Constance is allowed, but she is so prim and proper she will wait for us." Ellen wanted to apologize to Charles for her previous rash and rude behavior.

Charles winked and moved along, cleaning residents and helping them to finish their snacks while the other employees moved them to a different room.

Ellen sat with Constance and watched Maria holding on tightly to the armoire and screaming out, "I will get you bitches." The poised Catholic school teacher turned into a profane teacher, and instead of poetry she screamed out words no poet she ever knew wrote.

Maria Murphy, aka Emily Dickinson, forgot her teaching days and concentrated on this moment when she was finally ready to fight and escape to a place, although she was unsure where it was.

After ten minutes of putting up a fight, she calmed down from fatigue and not remembering what she was planning to do. She sat in the wheelchair, exhausted and shaking.

Constance moved next to her and held her hand, then whispered to Maria,
"Do not go gentle into that good night,
Old age should burn and rave at close of day,
Rage, rage against the dying of light."

Maria stirred and asked, "What did Dylan Thomas mean by rage against the dying light?
Was he addressing his father who was dying?"

Ellen and Constance looked at each other. Charles shook his head. They smiled at each other. Ellen got up, put her coffee cup in the garbage can, approached Charles, and said, "Thank you for the coffee."

Charles replied, "See you at happy hour on Friday. It is fun. And we have real booze!"

On Friday afternoons, the recreation department hosted happy hour with mocktails and cocktails. Thanks to donations from family members and well-wishers, they had a decent bar. This was an interaction space for families, too. They saw their lives in others' and took consolation in each other.

Ellen nodded and left without looking at Constance. She stopped at the nurse's station to tell them she was leaving. She faded down to the Exit door while Constance held on to Maria's hand. Maria snoozed as Charles put it, and Constance sat lost in her world, which might be real and disturbing.

Constance mused, *We talk and bemoan loneliness. Does Maria feel lonely and alone? Her half-open brain, mind, and being are still filled with her poets—the dead poets who give her company and remind her of her youth and productive life. They filled her life then and now.*

What does our sound mind make us feel? People talk about it and write about it for others to understand. When the sound mind slips off what do we feel? Who can say? Can research find out? Are we fine and feel safe? Or are we scared? Constance sat, lost in her new thoughts.

What is life worth living for if it is not worth it? Who says it is or it isn't! Each is worth its existence, the way it is. Savor it! Constance rationalized.

The Hudson was silent. No waves, just an occasional speed boat racing in the middle of the river. The far-away mountains had steam hovering over their heads. The greenery has started to genuflect, their tops weary from the heat.

Constance thought about the summer days in Lake George. She sat beside the lake on the slope behind the house. She remembered with amusement, *Why did I lean against the weeping willow when I read?*

The hot air filled the land. There will be no breeze. The water was as calm as a sleeping new born. Then, suddenly, a great blue heron swirling her long neck and seventy-nine-inch wings float up with a fish in her long beak and flies away. The serenity of the moment is disturbed. The water swirls around for minutes before it settles down. Constance loved great blue herons. Their fearlessness when they dove into the water and their fluttering wings left an aura of *I don't care.* Although they appeared selfish, they left a bundle of positive energy around them.

There were days like this when she took naps listening to the robins, tree sparrows, or horned larks.

Henry loved to talk about birds. There were days when he

joined a group of staunch birdwatching geeks. With his binoculars hanging around his neck, his gold glasses covered under his navy blue cap he set out for bird watching.

Memories and thoughts so fond to her, they haunted her at the stir of a familiar sight or sound. Reminiscing that leaves bleeding scars her soul will savor for days until another one of these recurs.

CHAPTER 11

The howling wind took its course outside the gray walls. Constance looked outside her window. The water in the Hudson was not visible. *It is really dark! Fall is here.*

Autumn was their favorite season. Henry and Constance stayed in their cottage in Lake George most of the fall weekends. Charles and William loved to play polo like their father. Edward was a hiker. He came home smothered in dirt and sweat at the end of the day with unusual plants, mushrooms, and wild berries. Constance was just happy that none of them were hunters. Sophia played tennis and rode her pony.

Dinnertime was the most fun of all. The children were allowed to eat "Without proper decorum," as Henry always said, because he wanted the days in the cottage to be fun. They ate together on the veranda in the back, overlooking the lake. Talking with their mouths full, laughing loudly, eating without napkins and proper utensils always excited them.

As they started to have their own families, the weekends were mostly Henry and Constance. They did not have any housekeepers there. Gardening was their passion. The autumn flowers excited them. She cut them and brought them inside and arranged them in an array of bounty.

They took long walks. Constance loved to pick perfect leaves she saw during those walks. They ate in small local restaurants. On Sunday evenings when they left Lake George, she filled her car with local produce. She baked pies and cakes with the fruits she brought back from Upstate New York. Autumn in New York is breathtaking!

She remembered the cobwebs, sans spiders, by the side

of the rails along the bridge she strolled across the vast lake. They were perfect, and they stood the torture of winter and the scorching heat of summer. *Sans the spiders!* The day after it rained, little drops of water stuck in between the threads of the web like little diamonds.

Are we the spiders who pass along our comfortable habitats we toil all our lives to build then pass on, leaving the perfect settings to Whispering Pines?

Where is my habitat? The shiny perfect castle I had with my husband and children is shattered.

Constance exhaled in agony. Or was it confusion and distress?

She wondered what the family who lived down the road from their cottage, the one with the red-headed daughter, might be doing now. Alfred and Stacy Conklin and their daughter! They are both teachers, and they lived there all year round. The year there was flooding in the cottage on a heavy winter day, they took care of it and they insisted Constance and Henry not drive in the dangerous weather.

When Constance did not show up with her children this fall, they might have called and her children might have said, "Mother is grieving," or "We insisted and she refused to come. Maybe soon." Phony answers with no essence. Their clouded statements masking the truth.

The last time she spoke to the Conklins was at Henry's funeral. They even brought the red-haired girl. Constance couldn't remember her name. Henry always called her "Redhead." She reminded him of the redheaded woodpecker, pounding in the woods behind their house. He used to laugh, "Here comes the feisty little woodpecker."

Constance wanted to write them a thank you note. She regretted neglecting that thought. It is almost time to start Christmas cards. She will add a detailed note with the card for the Conklins.

Constance wondered, *Will they come for my funeral? Will they bring the red head? Will any one notify them? So many wills!*

Her thoughts wandered back to Lake George. Lake George in autumn was exciting.

The change of colors, the first fire in the fireplace, and the smell of baking made her ecstatic with joy. The chill in the still air was relaxing. Of all her losses, the things she missed the most were autumn days on Lake George. She sighed and listened to the howling wind and sat still trying to erase her memories and sleep. Lately she envied the residents who had total memory loss.

The passage of time and life is never noticed until we meet a kid and we remember when they were born and they're standing in front of you with a spouse and a kid of their own, or until we count the missing familiar faces vanished from our lives.

Constance wondered, *Did I ever reflect on my past life? Now is the time. I am confined here with only time in my hand, which I never had. Am I up to it? To bring joys and hurts, failures and victories, pleasures and unpleasantness into my heart, churn up what I feel now?* She sighed. The sum of it all ran a chill down her spine. Just the thought, not the results.

Ruby peeked in. She saw Constance standing by the window, lost in thought. She came in and said, "Constance, you should be in bed. Do you know what time it is?" Constance smiled. Ruby fixed her bed and walked her to it. After tucking her in bed, she sang, "Amazing Grace."

Amazing Grace, How sweet the sound
That saved a wretch like me
I once was lost, but now am found
T'was blind but now I see
T'was Grace that taught my heart to fear
And Grace, my fears relieved
How precious did that grace appear
The hour I first believed
Through many dangers, toils and snares
We have already come.
T'was grace that brought us safe thus far
And grace will lead us home,
And grace will lead us home
Amazing grace, Howe Sweet the sound
That saved a wretch like me

I once was lost but now am found
T'was blind but now I see
Was blind, but now I see.

Constance glided into a relaxing, rhythmic breathing of peace and slowly drifted to her circadian sleep cycle. Ruby sighed. When she was done with her rounding and changing, before she sat down to document and chart, she came to check on Constance. Constance was often awake, either lost in her thoughts or reading. Ruby put her to bed and sang her to sleep. This had become a new routine for them.

Life! All that she has and is with her, she is not able to spare the pain of betrayal and rejection by her most valuable assets, her children. Ruby remembered that she had disliked Constance when she first met her. Her mere presence irritated her. Ruby knew she was rich beyond her comprehension. When she saw Anthony coming in to visit her, she was certain Constance was arrogant and still kept servants as slaves. The shock of all was when Ruby met Martha for the first time. Martha confided in Ruby her grief about the changes and the lost past Constance shared with her family.

Martha was Anthony's daughter, with a degree in law from Harvard. Constance, Ebony, Martha, and Anthony went to church on Sundays after she came to Whispering Pines. They even went to the Hamptons for a whole week!

Ruby remembered the night when Constance had her first panic attack after coming to Whispering Pines. The first few days Constance slept. She was irritated, threw things around, and slowly regressed to a phase of extreme moodiness, constantly crying. Then she slept at the end of each crying spell. The flat appeasement and air of arrogance buzzed off Ruby. Her children took turns visiting the first week. Sophia cried every time she came to see her mother. She placed expensive boxes of pastries at the nurse's station. Charles, William, and Edward visited the first weekend with their wives.

Anna Ritter wondered why they were all dressed as if going to a wedding. She mumbled under her breath, "For God's sake, it's a filthy nursing home. Retirement home, my arse." They spent more time talking to employees and management. Everybody was buried in their stories and supported them. The air around them looked green, bundled in the logo dollar signs.

At the first meeting the family held with the clinical team, Dr Ephraim, the medical director, wrote on Elizabeth Mann's note pad, "Crap. Something smells rotten."

Elizabeth replied, "You got it, Doc."

The clinical team read deeply into the children's minds. They were up to something vicious.

The social worker, talked about discharge planning. "Day one of admission starts discharge planning. Most of the time, the biggest hurdle is money. To have adequate care at home is the number-one priority."

Charles interjected, "Thinking about discharge at this time? Did you see the condition of our mother? Well, don't worry, we will make arrangements to move her elsewhere."

The rest of the meeting seemed vexatious, irked by clashing personalities. When the Italian leather on their shoes hit the floor in random unison motion, Constance sighed.

Sophie, with her wild blue eyes, looked at Constance as they wheeled her out of the conference room. She, the epitome of class and elegance, sitting like a lost soul!

Constance was perking up. Anthony and her lawyer were visiting her daily. Constance continued to stay quietly in her room. Anthony rearranged her room. He brought new books, writing materials, blankets, and clothes for Constance. Food and beverages were brought in. Anthony waited on her like her ever-faithful butler.

He took her outside and sat under the pine trees with her, covered in a shoulder-length vintage jacket as she watched the Hudson. That reminded her of the days when she and Henry sat silently, holding hands, watching and breathing a spring dusk or a fall afternoon as they indulged in the smooth rumble of the Hudson River.

Her love of the river was one of the reasons her children

chose Whispering Pines. The sights left behind were fading, and they were slipping away from her daily thoughts. The weeping willows and the pines pilfered through her mind. The early autumn birds—the yellow warblers and great crested flycatchers —she left in Lake George were replaced with the herds of sparrows pecking among the dry leaves on the ground.

Anthony noticed that her crying spells were lessening. Occasionally he noticed a fading smile. Her face was still sad and dry. Her eyes were fixed somewhere, and it seemed like she was trying to figure out what she saw, straining hard and failing.

He told Martha, "There is some progress. I don't know why she is refusing to appeal."

"Give her time to figure it out. Mrs. Sutton is smart."

Ruby talked to everyone at Whispering Pines about her daughter and her three children left in Jamaica and how, no matter what she tried, she was unable to bring them to the United States. She blamed the U.S. government. She blamed all the Americans who hated Islanders. And she blamed her sins and God punishing her, as per her pastor. Above all, she feared the devil was in the middle of it all. Her daughter was in danger the longer she stayed. Ruby feared her husband would hurt her daughter and children.

Life was cruel to her, and she verbalized it whenever she could. She talked to her colleagues. One night, Douglas Chester was working the night shift with Ruby. They were having their after first rounds tea. Doug made tea and saw Constance sitting in the lounge chair in front of the nurse's station. He looked around. Guiseppina was tucked up in a Geri chair, asleep.

Maybe it is a good night, Douglas thought. *I don't hear any rhythm of fast-moving wobbly legs, screaming, inaudible words, or shrieking bed alarms.*

Douglas extended Constance a cup of tea. "No thank you," she replied.

Ruby said, "Don't. She will not sleep with all the caffeine in her head."

Douglas pulled the chair forward and extended his legs on

the mantle, then stretched his body. He sipped his tea and said, "Ms. Ruby, I brought you good luck today. Everyone is sleeping."

Ruby shush'd him, "Bite your tongue."

Constance said, "The calmness before the threatening stormy turbulence."

Douglas replied, "Girl, you learning to talk!" He high fived her in the air. They started laughing. Ruby shushed them again.

Douglas said, "Grandma, why are you grumpy?"

Ruby sighed. She looked at Douglas and said, "I spoke to Rebecca, my daughter. Her man is going to kill her. I have no way of bringing her here. The lawyer from my church, he took all my money and no results. Child, it's killing me." The sadness and desperation in Ruby's eyes made Constance uneasy. She closed her book and got up.

"Constance, let me tuck you in." Ruby follower her.

Ruby's "Amazing Grace" was Constance's sleeping pill. The days when Ruby was off, Constance stayed in her bed, wide-awake, listening to the rustling pines and weeping willows. The birds cooing and nudging, the gentle lullaby of the Hudson, and the occasional commotions created by agitated patients in the hallway as the night dragged along.

When Ruby turned to shut the door, Constance said, "Don't worry. Everything will be alright."

CHAPTER 12

Autumn winds in their intensity swirled the ripened, rotten leaves and carried them away, maybe far away to lie in repose. Some of the heavy leaves cluttered around the trees. Constance looked outside. The starry autumn sky was brightly lit. The leaves left on the trees, dry and wrinkled and weary, were tortured by the strong wind.

If Maria was awake and she heard the howling wind, she would be singing "Ode to the West Wind." Or will she remember that?

The squirrels and chipmunks gnawing on pine nuts and hickory nuts had retreated to their habitats. During the day, they ran around working hard. Constance remembered the day that Edward was bit by a chipmunk. As usual, he was outside rummaging through the dry leaves. He had a stick in his hand. The small bushes were crushed by his stick. Edward saw a chipmunk crawling under a small heap of leaves on the sidewalk. He dug in and grabbed the chipmunk. Scared and trying hard to escape, the chipmunk bit the tip of his pinkie.

Edward tried to stop the bleeding without letting anyone know he had been bitten by a chipmunk. Henry noticed the dried bloodstains on his shirt at dinner. Henry and Constance had to get the Conklins to stay with the children and take Edward to the hospital. Even now Constance shuddered at the thought of the rabies shot. They had to hold him down while he screamed and kicked. Five shots in all. To this day, Edward will not leave a squirrel or chipmunk alone. He throws stones at them.

Constance wanted to start reading poetry again. After college, she never went back to reading poetry. The fact was that she never liked poetry. She was required to take a class at St Mary's.

Maria might have had a dreamy world, one that might be intact and fluid in her mind. How could I know?

The signs of the impending cold days of winter are in the making. When she daydreamed or stayed awake, her thoughts became disconcerted and a shade of green melancholy rattled and finally brought tears into her eyes.

The commotion outside woke her from her webbed musing. In the hallway, George was trying to calm Muriel and make her sit down in the wheelchair. She screamed, "Let me out. He is killing me! Leave me alone! He is a killer!" She looked exhausted and sweaty. She was panting, and saliva drooling off the side of her lips dripped on to her pink sweater.

George was hugging her tight, standing behind the wheel chair. His face was taut and tight with a rush of blood and his eyes begged, *God, help her, please.*

Residents sitting in their chairs dozing, restless people walking, and visitors trying to have quality time with their loved ones relaxing inside the solarium diverted their attention to George and Muriel.

Mirna fumbled, "God, all hell is going to let loose in seconds."

"Charles, can you come with me to the solarium? I might need you." Anna Ritter, the charge RN for the evening called out and then picked up her pace. Cynthia and Dolores followed.

"Get two more staff. We need to move people out to the activity room. I don't want the other residents to freak too," Anna continued. "Can the visitors please take your loved ones to the recreation room or the entrance room?"

Some had already started to do so. Others were waiting to absorb the situation and later interpret it in different ways, mainly at the residents' council. It was always a meeting tainted with their own perception of what happened and what would have happened if the staff were different. This was the place to complain about the staff, God forbid they thought they were not right for their loved one. It happens over and over, and the dedicated staff pretend they have not heard about it.

Minty Weinberg started screaming, "Kill him before he hurts her!" She lunged at George with her shaky arms and unsteady legs.

Mirna was right in time to block her fall. She caught her and sat her down on her chair. She said, "Minty, what is going on? Let's get out of here. Let's go for a walk."

Stubborn and agitated, Minty got out of the chair. "No, no. I will kill him before he kills her. No killing her." Minty folded her hands.

"Stubborn old fart," Charles whispered and moved forward to Minty. "Mrs. Weinberg," he said, "Let's go for a stroll. Take my hand."

She held his hand as she tumbled toward the door. In her new frame of mind, Minty loved men. Her explicit sexual connotations stunned her daughter. As per her daughter, "We wondered how we were born out of her. We have never heard her talk about sex or act like she ever had sex." She turned to her husband and said, "Mom used to bully us to wear pantyhose all the time." They laughed.

Well, thoughts, when clouded and plagued in their despondency, turn to thoughts eroded through the layers and hit the spot to arouse unknown suppressed fragments. They might travel and hit forsaken areas. Who can say what it is? Minty's daughter has noticed the change in her character since her mother was diagnosed with dementia.

Constance walked back to her room. She gazed outside. The weeping willow spread out its wings in the evening sun. Such an enchanting sight. She wished for Henry to be near her, sitting together by the lake, watching the sun set and holding hands. As the sun vanished behind the mountain, revealing the foliage doused in a shimmering golden glaze, they walked home along the creek. The leaves falling into the creek led to small swirls made by bass playing in the clear, cold water.

Henry loved to skip stones across the water. With a sly grin on his tight lips, he would hold me tighter. These were dreams we lived once upon a time.

Dreaming and wishing, Constance fell into a restless nap. When she woke up, she saw an illegible contour on the wall. A chill shivered through her spine. Unable to move, she lay in bed, shivering. And then everything disappeared. She laughed. The redheaded wood pecker at the window, reflected on the wall as a scary vision.

It is dark outside. The moon is shining, giving a clear view of the outside. The pines exuded a sense of belonging. They whispered to Constance that she belonged here. She heard the whisper of the pines in her dreams. Her dreams were shattered by distrust, fear, hopelessness, and—occasionally—unfathomable guilt.

Ms Ruby's "Amazing Grace" echoed in the hallways, drifting her off to serenity. Constance relaxed. Her mind and body eased as if she had a Xanax. She nudged her head on the pillow. A lonely nightingale called out to her mate, parent, or child. The far cry echoed through the pines, swirled around the weeping willows, and floated off into the Hudson.

The last resident was tucked in safely, and the last lights were turned off. The gray walls of Whispering Pines stood guard around them. The far cry of the nightingale boomeranged through the woods.

CHAPTER 13

Barren trees and their forsaken, dried leaves lying withered on the ground. Blue jays flying around and sparrows pecking on leftover seeds gave the aura of autumn in all its majesty and fury is taking its bow and disappearing behind the curtain.

Constance remembered, *This means, Thanksgiving is around the corner.*

My first Thanksgiving without Henry!

Maria peeked in and Constance said, "Hello, Maria. How are you?" In some ways, Maria made her uncomfortable. Her lack of knowledge of poetry embarrassed her. After all, Constance took four years of poetry at St Mary's Academy and never read a line of poetry after graduation.

What a shame! She smiled. *Whoever thought I would have to meet this challenge during this decade of my life.*

It seemed distressing compared to meeting her kids after they placed her at Whispering Pines. Martha had brought her books of poetry at her request.

Staring at the last days of the season, Maria recited,
"Lo! Sweeten'd with the summer light,
The full-juiced apple, waxing over-mellow,
Drops in a silent autumn night.
All its allotted length of day"
Maria looked at Constance. Constance knew it was a Tennyson poem, "The Lotus Eaters," and she grabbed her collection of poems and turned pages. Before Maria screamed, she read,
"The flower ripens in its place,
Ripens and fades, and falls, and hath no toil,
Fast-rooted in the fruitful soil"

Maria sat next to Constance. She laid her right hand on Constance's lap. She looked into Constance's eyes, as if she expected more.

Constance stared outside with Maria. She didn't know what was going through Maria's mind. Constance mourned the loss of her colorful autumn, and with that thought came the crumbling and fading aspirations of her present life.

Maria suddenly stood up and walked away, after spending an hour in deep solitude with Constance. She wandered on to Longfellow,

It was Autumn, and incessant
Piped the quails from shocks and sheaves
And, like living coals, the apples
Burned among the withering leaves

Constance was relieved when Maria left the room. She had no clue what she was saying. She thought, *It is no wonder the family called her Emily Dickinson.*

Whispering Pines woke up to a new day. It was Constance's first Thanksgiving without Henry. Yesterday she lay in bed sleepless, just thinking. She heard the hushed voices of nurses and nursing assistants, the first staff around after six a.m., waking residents.

They used to joke, "Mornings are better, no sundowning." Charles called mornings "The peaceful hour."

The inaudible loud words of residents mixed with the soft discourse of the staff, sounds of closing doors and dragging wheelchairs, persisted for hours. Constance absorbed the mixed noises and stretched in her bed in a vague attempt to wake up. She took her watch from the side table to check the time. Her eyes caught the date, November 28, Thursday, on her Rado. She gasped, *My first Thanksgiving without Henry!*

Sulking back into her pillow, weak with dejection and desolation, Constance tried to recall the clatter of silverware, the smell of roasting turkey, and the contented laughter. Whispering Pines was offering a Thanksgiving Dinner for residents and their families around 11.30 a.m. That would give families the opportunity to spend part of the day with the residents and still gather with loved ones for their festivities later, without gloom or guilt.

Constance had received the invitations to send out to loved ones, inviting them to share the day of Thanksgiving at Whispering Pines. She knew her children were gathering at Lake George, as per their tradition. She did not get an invite to join them.

Anthony had suggested, "Let's go to Lake George. We will spend Thanksgiving there. You need a change. I know you love it there."

Constance bit her lower lip and shook her head, " No, Anthony the children are planning to go there. I can't."

Anthony noticed that she appeared fragile and ready to shatter at the slightest breath.

"What about the Hamptons? Or even Westchester?"

"Maybe this year we'll have Thanksgiving with our new friends," Constance replied.

She was not surprised she had not received an invitation from any of her friends. Thanksgiving was always a private affair for the Suttons, contrary to Christmas celebrations.

The Suttons gave their employees a whole week off. Even Anthony spent Thanksgiving with Ebony and Martha. It was their time as a family. They travelled to Lake George the weekend before Thanksgiving. The kids were taken out of school, and they carried their school work with them.

Constance ordered her farm-fresh turkey the minute she reached the house. Once the order was placed she would sigh, turn to Henry, and say, "Oh dear, half the work is done."

Henry would laugh in between his Scotch and say, "Oh dear, Mother has started Thanksgiving."

Constance would twirl and turn and wink at him.

They biked and hiked and sat by the fire outside and talked. Constance cherished those moments. She would give her life to be there right now. She can't, though, and that is the reality. She thought about her Thanksgiving menu. She made a lemon herb-roasted turkey. The recipe was given to her by her great aunt. The day before Thanksgiving, she marinated her turkey and left it on the countertop. She made homemade cranberry sauce from scratch and molded it in a crystal bowl.

The next step was to make a cranberry Champagne cocktail. Chilled and poured into a crystal flute, it was soooo refreshing. She sipped her drink while peeling potatoes for mashed potatoes and making the pumpkin puree for pumpkin pie. She also made sure she made her apple pie crust. She did not believe in making too much food.

"We have to be thankful for what we have and give to the needy. God has blessed us immensely, beyond doubt abundantly," she told the children.

The last task before retiring for the day was setting the Thanksgiving table. A couture handmade vintage white lace cloth adorned her mahogany custom-made dining table. She made her centerpiece with pinecones, colorful leaves, fall vegetables, and fruits. She accented it with candles. Royal Doulton tableware set in order, Bohemia crystalware, and sparkling cutlery sets adorned her table. She enjoyed every minute of it.

Joining her family on the porch cuddled in Henry's arms, listening to nature and her family engulfed her in harmony. The yellow warblers relaxed in their nests and the crickets and fireflies snoozed in the crisp late-autumn air.

The day of Thanksgiving, she woke up around 5 a.m. to the orderly chirping of yellow- bellied sapsuckers. The red- headed woodpecker drummed on the oak tree for its prey. The first cup of coffee and kneading dough for Parker house rolls was accompanied by making cornbread. By the time the sky turned orange and red, Constance was out on her regular run. The dew on the grass and leaves brushing her face, she inhaled deeply, as if it was her last breath.

The sweetness of pure nature filled her lungs and energized her. She was thankful in every way, filled with gratitude as she passed the Conklins, who are away in Brooklyn with their family. The squealing gurgles of the wild creek cheered her on. What an amazing way to start Thanksgiving and gratitude on this special day.

Constance stood back and inspected her Thanksgiving table before she went to take a shower and change. Perfectly roasted herb lemon turkey adorned the turkey platter, surrounded by dishes filled with cranberry sauce, mashed potatoes, baked sweet potatoes, and grilled mixed vegetables. Pumpkin pie and apple pie rested on the kitchen counter to be served with homemade whipped cream.

She could hear Henry and the boys watching football. When Constance peeked in, Henry said, "Ready?"

He got up and opened the first bottle of Dominique Lafton Meursault, her favorite Chardonnay. And the festivities started. Fun, laughter, and Thanksgiving gratitude filled the room and minds of a strong-clad family. Henry always let Constance carve the turkey. She did it in style, while Henry poured Boisset-clos de la Roche Grand Cru. The ruby red color of the wine dazzled in her crystal glass.

Dessert was in front of the TV. Henry helped clean up and, as Constance made herself comfortable on the sofa, Henry reinforced the fire and drew a blanket over her feet. And the best was a glass of Viagnier to go with her pies. Savoring every drop, she used to say Thanksgiving prayers for the abundance filling her life.

The door opened and Dolores Cooper said, "Wake up, sleepyhead. Let me fix you a cup of coffee." She moved in to use the coffee machine. Dolores turned around and said, "Do you mind if I have a cup of your good coffee? I am exhausted. I woke up at 2 a.m. and did all the cooking. I will be home, barely, 5 p.m."

Constance smiled and shook her head, "Any time, my dear."

Dolores said, "This is your first Thanksgiving here. Oh my! The commotion, families and residents. I can't wait for the day to end. On top of that, unlike other holidays, all of the big shots from administration will be here."

Dolores left with a steaming cup of coffee. Constance wondered, *Why do I stay awake at night, unable to sleep? What do other people worry about? How many stay awake at night worrying?*

Constance never had to worry about finances.

Some fear about their next meal, some about a roof over their head, some about a loved one. Now Constance spends countless sleepless nights over her failure as a mother. Most of the residents here are sleepless due to unknown fears that are unclear to them, a fate they carry as their disease progresses. Constance faded into a rainbow of thoughts in front of her meal.

Anthony, Ebony, and Martha joined Constance at Whispering Pines. She held conversations with residents and their families. Anthony had brought her favorite Viognier. They had a drink before dinner, which relaxed her, and later Constance would have another with Ebony's mixed berry pie.

They escorted Constance back to her room when the meal was finished.

CHAPTER 14

The first snowflakes rolled around. Constance opened her window and inhaled the chill in the air. Dewy white snow swirled at her face and a few flakes landed on her eyelids and nose. She stretched her tongue to capture a few more flakes. Ms. Ruby came in on her midnight rounds and placed her hands on her hips. "What are you doing? Want to catch pneumonia. It is freezing, child." She moved hastily toward Constance, then led her away from the window and closed it.

"Can I make you some tea?" Ruby asked.

"No, thank you. I am okay. I will lie down and see if I can doze off." Constance sat on her bed and shook her head to affirm to Ruby that she was alright.

Ruby tucked Constance into her bed, the smooth blanket and soft pillows smothered under her. Celine Matthews, the night nurse, came in and waved her hand, whispering, "Is everything all right, Constance?"

Constance whispered back, "Fine, thank you."

Miss Ruby stood by the head of the bed and sang "Amazing Grace." The depth of the song brought tears to Celine's eyes. She closed her eyes and absorbed the spiritual nourishment.

"Let's go," Celine whispered to Ruby when she opened her eyes. She looked at Constance. Her eyes were closed and the gentle up and down movement of her chest was even. They walked out half hugging, closed the door and walked toward the nurse's station.

Constance savored the reverence of a peaceful sleep. As she sank deeper into her pillow, she felt Henry next to her. His arms were wrapped around her shoulders and stomach. His breath warmed her. The subconscious was already filled with her favorite snowflakes. The unconscious mind started to be nourished by Henry's presence. Constance sighed in contentment as the circadian rhythm picked up. The blessing of a good night's peaceful sleep drowned her into oblivion.

"Miss Ruby, what did you do to Celine to make her cry?" Victoria Stewart was pouring tea into cups, adding sugar and milk for her colleagues.

They huddled together, reported on patients, and concentrated on documentation. Louis Martin was sitting at the nurse's station on a recliner chair covered in blankets. Celine checked his chair alarm before sitting down at her desk. Louis opened her eyes and stared at the nurses, then struggled to get up. Celine went up to her and massaged her hands, which he stretched out to get the anchorage to go up. Celine kept on gently massaging his hands, and he laid back and closed his eyes. She tucked him in an extra blanket to Ruby's demand, "Child, cover him good. I don't want him to catch a cold."

Celine Matthews smiled. The rough Ruby has the warmest heart. Patients loved her. They listen to her commands – strict orders coated with steel and a smooth sugar mush inside. Have to love her!

"Tea time, Miss Ruby," chimed Victoria

"Thank you, Gabriella," said Ruby.

"Until coffee time at five," Gabriella laughed. "Why were you upset?"

She turned to Celine.

"Just the patients. Watching their lives upsets me at times. How our amazing life can turn to havoc just because of mad, roaring waves that are rushing in all the wrong ways." Celine wiped her tears again.

They sat in silence, concentrating on their work while studiously listening for bells, alarms, and unusual noises. Swirls of snow dwindled down the weeping willows and pines. The Hudson tickled by, the snow flurries rose and fell into ecstasy as it moved forward in harmony. The river banks slept wrapped in the white snow blanket.

The early morning nurse's station was unusually busy. The phones were ringing with inquiries from administration about the status! They wanted to know if patients were sleeping, if emergency supplies were in place, and, of course, the morning staffing.

Ruby mumbled "Why are they bothering us? If one more call wakes Martin, they're hearing from me. Me curse them."

When Ruby started ranting, she used her Jamaican slang expressions, which caused an uproar of laughter at the nurse's station. Ruby put her index finger on her lips. "Sshssh!"

"These child make me slave now," She stood up, put her charting on the table, and started her hourly rounds.

Victoria whispered, "Sit. I will do it." Ruby kept walking down the hallway.

Maria was walking down the hall. Victoria guided her toward the nurse's station. She strolled along and went into the solarium. The wind was roaring and bumping into the windows. The cracking sound was annoying and scary. Maria parted the curtains and peeked outside. The snow was fiercely flashing on the pines and the sides of the building. Maria watched the outside with curiosity. Victoria stood at the door and stayed with Maria.

Maria started to pace, and Victoria knew she was getting outside her comfort zone. She called out to Celine, just enough for her to hear, "Some dead poet has to show up or else we will be in trouble."

Celine approached her and said, "Maria, do you need tea?"

Maria was busy thinking. Her face was crumbled, lips pursed, and eyes were pinpoint. She needed to be diverted to another zone. When she was out of control, the whole floor was disturbed. Celine stood with her and gently said, "Do you like snow?"

Maria stood motionless, and Celine's question made no waves in her brain cells. Celine continued, "Maria, I had no snow in India. So I am very crazy about snow. So pretty." Celine's hands rubbed Maria's shoulders gently. She could feel the tight muscles slowly relaxing. Maria sighed.

"Maria, you okay?"

Maria's cold muscles warmed up under Celine's gentle touch. Maria, lost in her entangled world, forgot what she was untangling. Maybe a forgone thought, maybe a word of wisdom to the staff, or maybe a favorite poem!

Celine steered Maria toward the nurse's station. They walked with baby steps.

Victoria had tea in her hand. She helped Maria to take her first sip. She took the teacup and sipped. She watched the rising steam evaporating from her teacup. She warmed up to the tender environment the staff built around her for the moment. Maria stretched in the reclining chair, and Maria positioned her comfortably and went to get her blanket. Maria looked out and mumbled,

"It sifts from leaden sieves
It powders all the wood,
It fills with alabaster wool
The wrinkles of the road."

"Do you know the rest?" Maria turned to Celine.

Celine smiled and said, "No, ma'am."

Maria fought hard to remember the rest and Celine knew she had to divert her to another topic. Before it happened, Maria screamed and got up tangled in her blanket, running down the hallway and dragging it with her. Staff could not stop her. Celine went inside the medication room to get her medicine and joined Ruby and Victoria, who were behind Maria, a foot away to catch her if she fell with just enough space between them not to scare her.

When Maria reached her room, the staff held her and placed her on her bed. Maria kicked and screamed, "Help, they're killing me. Help, help!"

Ruby said, "Come on, Matthews, I am tired. Where is the medicine, child?" She sat on the bed and leaned against Maria to stabilize her. Victoria held Maria tight, making sure she was not hurting her from the opposite side.

The pinch of the needle, the sting of Haldol, the hands holding her in her bed scared her. Maria wiggled her legs and hands and tried to get up. Her scream resonated like a plea for her memory to come back, and the hate flowing out of her was toward her plaqued brain to explode and replace it with new cells. Or was it at the whole process of no turning back and taking another route to her golden years while cherishing fond memories of a victorious past?

The rotten golden years of the present moment slowly vanished away as Maria slid off to sleep. It was the best thing for her right now. The hands holding her loosened, and they wrapped her in her blanket and positioned her with pillows. The side rails went up.

Celine checked the bed alarm and sighed. Ruby stayed back, folding Maria's hair to the side and brushing sticking layers of hair from her face. She took a wash cloth and wiped her sweaty face. Maria stirred and opened her eyes. Her cloudy, weary eyes squinted to focus on Ruby and rolled back. In a second her breathing was even and rhythmic. Her face loosened. Peaceful sleep engulfed her woes, fear, and confusion. Hours of bliss smiled at her. The luxury of deep, mindless sleep!

Ruby checked the bed alarm again and left Maria alone to sleep.

Celine Matthews knew she needed an evaluation for Maria. Maria was getting more forgetful. Her medications and her care plan have to be looked at. She made a referral for Dr. Ephraim.

The morning light peeked through the snow and tried to show their face. Snow had taken its strength, and the wind picked up at times. The windows were covered in pure white. Constance woke up. It took her a few minutes to fathom that she was not in charge of getting help to move the snow from the long driveway or pathways leading to the stables and the pond.

She no longer had to make sure she provided coffee and breakfast to all the workers.

CHAPTER 15

Christmas rolled over in royal splendor. The busy world became busier and busier. The weary ones became wearier and tired of the season by the beginning of December. They counted days to go, gifts to buy, and parties to arrange and attend.

Staff at Whispering Pines transformed themselves into little elves.

The Miracle of Christmas!

Whispering Pines plunged into their own part in the celebration of holidays. The decorations were taken out of storage: Christmas, Hanukkah, and Kwanza. Christmas decorations always took precedence. Well, Constance wondered if any one cared, or noticed, or complained about any of the festivities. Kids coming to sing carols from churches and schools was the favorite for most residents. Some sang along, some stared into space, some fidgeted to get loose and wander. The ones who were able to walk independently wandered of their own free will.

Some children clung to their parents, puzzled and wondering about what they were seeing, scared of the impact on life as time passes. Complacent as they could be, they sang carols and scurried off with their parents to their little lives outside the gray walls. The red and green lights strung in harmony on the trees and gray walls did not kindle little sparks in their tender minds. Life outside the walls was more colorful without imperfections in their thoughts.

Constance knew from the perplexed faces that they were perturbed about what they saw. Their grandparents, if alive, were at home, making cookies and showering them with gifts for the holidays. Constance missed her grandchildren. She mourned

Christmas time now, this was not the way she had celebrated Christmas in the past.

The recreation staff had candy canes for the carolers. Constance opened the little bag she had in her lap. She brought out dainty boxes in gold and handed each one of the carolers: Godiva chocolate. The little faces lit up. Parents cheered. The little eyes cannot believe their gifts. When Constance heard about the carolers, she had ordered the chocolate from her favorite chocolatier.

The red-haired girl in her green holiday outfit smiled and said, "Thank you."

Constance thought about her red-haired woodpecker. The Conklins might have already received her Christmas card and the gift basket she had sent them. She ordered good quality wine, cheese, candy, and a doll to be included in the basket.

The Jacques Torres chocolate Anthony's daughter had brought Constance was half finished already, and Christmas was still thirteen days away. A naughty twinkle brightened her eyes.

Naughty as she was to Henry, her face crumbled in sadness. She said to herself, *Get back to your room, you know what to do.*

Minty Weinberg started clapping, and Minnie Blackwood shook her head and slapped her thighs as most of the staff and residents clapped and thanked the little carolers. Hal Blum walked up to them and shook hands with parents and whichever little ones dared enough to be brave. Others hid behind their parents.

As the delicious Jacques Torres chocolate melted in her mouth, drowning away the upsurging emotions surfacing from her stomach that stuck in her throat, Constance sighed. She looked at the frozen Hudson. No visible movement of life. She could not spot any Canadian geese, great blue heron, or ring-billed heron that wandered around on the water beds of the Hudson. They might be sheltered somewhere away from the cold, or frolicking in harmony with their mates.

The stillness of the Hudson is so powerful, Constance thought as she inhaled the stillness and calmness of a forlorn winter Saturday afternoon, alone in her room reminiscing about memories that are both painful and reassuring at the same time.

On the twenty-third of December, the residents had their holiday party. There was holiday music, played by a band. Extra staff was scheduled to manage the residents to and from and during the party. The glasses of red-colored punch looked really festive. Visitors, family members, and some residents were offered wine. There was sparkling cider, too.

Madison McGregor, one of the administrative staff, approached Constance and asked, "Mind if I get you a drink?"

Cheap wine always gave her a migraine headache. Gracefully declining, she said, "I have to drive, sorry."

Madison laughed and said, "Good one, Constance."

Anthony and Ebony were Constance's guests. They looked at each other. At Christmas celebrations, Henry opened bottles of Veuve Clicquot LaGrande Dame or Chateau Lafito, Constance's Christmastime favorite. There was always Sonoma-Cutrer Chardonnay, which Constance called "Crisp and silky in my mouth," and laughed a lot after a glass or two. In all the years Anthony had spent with the Sutton family, he had never seen Henry or Constance drunk and out of control. They never woke up in the morning with puffy red and glaring eyes. They did not drink their coffee with churning, sour bellies. They were special in every way.

Anthony choked on his ginger ale. Ebony felt his pain, and she squeezed his hands under the table and said, "Breathe. Slow down, dear." Anthony wiped his face and tried to smile.

Henry Sutton used to say, "Hey, bourbon man, have a glass of this." Anthony hated those expensive wines. Wine burned his throat, but not the bourbon.

Anthony looked at Constance, sitting poised, a smile on her face. Anthony felt the tumultuous currents striking and swirling in her mind. He got up and excused himself from the table. He went outside on the entrance porch. Ralph waved at Anthony and he waved back.

The entrance porch was empty except for Ralph and his assistant, at the security desk. The cold air was soothing. The leftover snow on the side of the driveway was muddy and black from dirt mixed with tire marks, and had already lost its pretty sanctity, like the lives he had just left behind.

The fading light in the sky painted faint yellow amidst dark gray and blue. White clouds moved around in unison. The white heron flying solo looked so small, like a lost sparrow.

Everyone received gifts—a sweater of the same color and different sizes packed in shiny wrapping paper that the widowed volunteers made sure were done perfectly. Names were neatly written, and the sweaters sized properly. Mindy Weinberg threw her sweater at Guiseppina and walked away. Cynthia walked with her to make sure she was safe until she reached her room and sat on her recliner. Cynthia turned the TV on for her.

Ruth Fisher was quiet during the party. Francine helped around with George and Katherine. After the party, George and Katherine were going out for a drink. George had told the staff they were "Just friends," and that they see each other occasionally. Constance believed life has various twists and turns, and we are entitled to follow the path that leads us to happiness. Danny and Molly sat next to Maria. Katherine walked up and hugged them both.

Guiseppina, looked around. Luigi and Bill smiled. She drank her cranberry juice silently.

To the staff's credit, the party was a success. The extra staff stood vigil to jump in and intervene for any need. When Minnie lifted her skirt and her hands wandered off, she was elegantly redirected to help with serving apple cider. She walked around asking, "Miss, can I do anything for you?"

Hal Blum was happily eating and drinking. He looked at Albert Crowley who was dozing. The food in front untouched. Charles sat next to him and started feeding him.

Annabel sat quietly. Amanda walked around helping. She looked at her mother. The queen of Christmas has a blank expression on her face.

All twenty-three residents attended the party dressed in their best clothes. The hard work the staff had to put in was rewarded. There were no mishaps, except a couple of outbursts and Mindy Weinberg's angry exit. Family members and volunteers sat down with tensed shoulders in anticipation of commotion, but as time passed they eased themselves with a drink, mostly nonalcoholic, to mimic their loved ones. Small gestures of love!

Hal complained, "This scotch on the rocks is too strong for me." He lifted his apple juice with ice in front of Doug and said, "You are a lousy bartender. I am not tipping you."

"Hal, can you recommend a good bartender," Doug asked. Hal winked.

Ellen Monroe stayed with Nadia next to Simon and Agatha, She waved at Ms Baker.

Fr. Sean arrived on Christmas Eve.

Maria walked around as if she was anticipating Advent and looking for a Merry Christmas. Father Sean was visiting mainly because his mother was ill. She was battling end-stage cancer. The last he had heard was that his mother had been placed on hospice.

Childhood memories of Christmas surged in his mind. He pictured Aunt Maria reading "'Twas the Night before Christmas" and his favorite, "Rudolph, the Red Nosed Reindeer." Uncles, aunts, and cousins coming together on Christmas Eve, singing carols and exchanging gifts.

Maria Murphy smiled looking at the mistletoe. Sean watched her. His aunt's face looked bare, like the trees outside. Even in her smile, the virility of her humanity waned without any lust for life. The crispiness of the air around her stood frozen in her gaze. The coldness around her aura was chilly. No tantalizing sparks to speak of! Her smile looked as if it came from a place far away from her heart, the heart which lost its symphony. Amazing as it is, it still held her vast abyss of poetry!

How could it be? Fr. Sean had gone over it so many times. He was discombobulated and mystified that Maria still had moments of poetic outbursts. No one could decide whether the origin of her thoughts were sourced from a normal, functioning brain or if it was an automated impulse. Unpredictable Aunt Maria.

Either way, the poetic self-portrayed Maria they knew years

ago, sans the lively passion she exhibited in her old world of poetry.

"Aunty Maria, do you want to attend midnight Mass?" Sean asked.

Maria started walking without answering him.

As snow started to fall and embrace the earth for a white Christmas, Sean left Whispering Pines to participate at the midnight Mass at St. Katherine's.

As he drove without Maria tailing him, he thought, *This might be the last Mass I will see my mom when I look from the pulpit.*

He wanted Maria to be there too, the whole family together one last time. It would have done some good for Maria's memory.

Fr. Sean said to himself, *I will try tomorrow to bring Maria home for dinner. Danny and Molly can help.*

CHAPTER 16

The hallway stripped of Christmas decorations, minus visitors and well-wishers, left a distinct air of gloom. The world outside the gray walls froze in the winter weather. Constance looked outside and wondered, *Are the seasons a portrait of my mood?*

She smiled, and Ms Ruby turned to her and said, "What are you smiling about? You want to share it with me"? Ruby was passing through the hallway and turning to check on Maria.

"Just the weather and my mood"!

Ruby laughed and remarked, "What a thought"!

The roaring snow and wind have subsided. Just the bone chilling cold! The walls of Whispering Pines blocked them from the freezing cold outside and offered what little warmth they could. The body is warm, but the soul is frozen!

Constance looked around for Maria. *Maybe she knows a dead poet or poetess who has a lyric for the occasion.*

Blum passed Constance in the hallway. He was in a hurry. He stopped at the nurse's station and talked to Elizabeth Mann, and then turned to the solarium. He might have asked the same question again, "I have molested so many women in the army. I am scared. Really, really scared. What am I to do?"

His hands were shaking. When he got very nervous, they handed him a small pill with a cup of water. They waited until he swallowed it, walked with him, and let him lie down in his room. When he came out after hours of staying in the room, he is calm and he smiles. He might be sleeping. Constance never peeked in his room or asked anyone about it. *Privacy is a privilege and an entitlement, which people seldom remember or oblige! How many of us are privy to these rights? Life turns around rules and rights to a point where we churn selfish thoughts to spin right and wrong as we wish!*

Constance smirked. The one privilege no one could ever steal from her is her cherished thoughts.

All the people here are holding on to their hidden dreams, fears, hopes, and hopelessness. No one else can extract them and enjoy those like I do.

Hal Blum went back to his room and settled himself in his bed. He covered his head with the blanket. He dreamed that he was driving in the sleet outside. The road under the icy surface left marks from sliding hither and there. A speeding car passed him. He was dwelling deep into his private dreams and a discreet smile creeped into the left corner of his lips. The speeding car passed him again.

What was that flash of light blinding me? What made me smile?

I don't remember now. Maybe I will remember later, and maybe never!

A wave of anger, hopelessness, anguish, and fear brewed inside, concocted into a dark elixir. Despair? Fear? Anxiety? Blum winced in his sleep. His eyelids fluttered, unable to open.

Hal Blum's mind rolled around the blank walls, rummaging for clues. Lost and confused, he became restless. He was still driving in the sleet. As his anger built up inside, he pressed on the pedal. He heard a distant honking, which woke him up.

Hal sat up, puzzled by the gray walls surrounding him. He walked up to the window. He saw the weeping willows and the pines and a glimpse of the river bordering the trees. He waited, staring at the dead silence surrounding him. He did not know what he was waiting for! Hal stared at the ceiling and saw a dark mark on the left corner.

As he kept staring, he saw it moving, turning into a dark line and then into circles.

Hal wondered, *Are there small wings on the dark circle?* Then the wings fluttered. Hal sprang up and grabbed the paper neatly folded in a file marked "Whispering Pines."

"What is Whispering Pines?" He could not concentrate. He saw the circle on the ceiling moving again. He jumped, waving the bulk of loose sheets wildly at the moving circle.

The papers flew everywhere. The circle with wings crawled forward, faster and faster. Blum shuddered. A cold chill ran through his body.

What is happening?

Then he heard the gunshot and the shout, "Get those scoundrels."

He sprang out, "Yeahhhhh!"

His lungs blew up with air. His brain bubbled and his body morphed into a Fight me, I'll get you mode.

With the folder marked Whispering Pines as his weapon, he charged outside, pushing the unlocked door open. He screamed, "I will get you bitches." The red alert went into full mode.

Mirna and Lisa ran toward Blum. They summoned Douglas and Charles to help them. Charles came out of the employee lounge. "Ladies, hold on. Let me help. Watch out, Hal is in rare form," he said.

Charles looked back to see if anyone heard him say rare form. Slang was no-no when it concerned residents and was serious enough for disciplining. He chuckled.

Blum heard loud voices, mixed with calm soothing ones, and one special voice topping it all.

"Mr. Blum, you are safe. You are at Whispering Pines."

Hal felt people grabbing him.

What?

Which part of Vietnam is Whispering Pines?

Who is here?

Hal's mind raced a million miles, riled up with a thousand thoughts.

He strained his eyes to look around for his friends.

None around!

"The civilians got me and they pinned me down."

Hal fought them all with zest and primal energy oozing from every pore in his body.

Charles and Douglas Chester held him tight and walked him back to his room. Hal resisted with all his strength, as if to reach the window and look outside for help. Through the fog outside, he saw barely visible skyscrapers in their glory under the starlit sky. They were unrecognizable, as he strained to open his eyes.

Charles and Douglas eased him to his bed. He felt spent and tired. His tight body slowly relaxed. He heard a familiar voice that said, "Breathe in and out. You are okay. I am here."

His mind eased and he closed his eyes. He does not remember for how long. When he felt someone staring at him, he opened his eyes. He saw the smiling face of Elizabeth Mann.

"Liz," Hal whispered.

"Drink some water. Your lips are dry." She brought the plastic glass to his lips and helped him to sit up. He sighed, perplexed and baffled. His unsettled dreams and thoughts had left him. He did not remember what happened before.

CHAPTER 17

The golden rays of the setting sun cast shadows on the gray walls of Whispering Pines. The majestic rays gave way to fading bizarre lines and shades. The unbalanced commotion of nature settling around the imbalanced molecules of Mr. Blum's thought process. He looked far ahead to the highway beyond the hills on the farther side of the Hudson.

Constance wrapped in a spring sweater wandered outside. The tree sparrows chirped in unison and flew around playfully in flocks. She inhaled the spring air—light and refreshing, surrounded by sprouting green vegetation. Constance spotted an eastern phoebe, migrating back after winter, looking amazed at the green layers of new life. The first signs of spring.

George and Katherine waved at Constance. She smiled. They were sitting on the patio chair with Muriel. They were sipping coffee and talking. They looked relaxed and happy.

The ways we live our lives beyond our wildest imagination! Constance wrote in her mind.

Spring has filled the void of the recently bare trees with thick, green foliage. The road behind the river is barely visible. Mr. Blum strained to look farther. He adjusted his glasses. The foggy shadows made no sense to him. His frustration stirred ripples of despair inside his brain. His arms started to shake. He started to rock back and forth, desperately trying to hug a stable object in his mind to put an anchor in front of the torrents leading him to the depths of destruction.

The unknown depth of uncertainty scared him.

Stomping on the floor, he stood up quickly. The intensity of his body movements and racing, tumultuous mind pushed him forward in an imbalance. The thud his body made as he hit the concrete wall startled Dolores. She ran out and called, "Mr. Blum is on the floor. Jesus, I don't know what happened."

The nursing staff running. Anna Ritter blurted out directions on her way to the patio, catching her breath in between running and calling for the code cart. She shouted, "Put the oxygen on. Vital signs please."

The nurse tried to pump the blood pressure cuff. Blum's hands lay limp at his sides.

"Hal, wake up." Ms. Baker nudged his chest.

Ms. Baker was sweating profusely. The agony of her obese body huddled on the floor uncomfortably and the instinct of a nurse smelling danger made her pale.

"He is not breathing," cried Elizabeth.

She tried to wiggle his limbs. She nudged his face. Then the chest rub.

"Call 911." Ms. Baker turned to Linda. Despite the uncomfortable situation, she was in total control.

"Code Blue. Start CPR."

Elizabeth started to pound on his chest in rhythmic beats. She mumbled, "Are we sure he is not a DNR?"

Hal Blum was still, a content smirk lingering on his blue face as if he was saying, *Finally, I am at peace. I am resting. I am not afraid anymore of my haunting memories. My anguish has faded. The relentless torture I endured for a lifetime has ended. They vanished into the setting sun.*

"No pulse. Continue CPR," Ms. Baker yelled.

Dr. Ephraim came running. His quick steps echoed his urgency to get to the scene and take charge.

"Stop CPR. I am pronouncing Hal. Technically, it is time." He looked at his watch.

Ms. Baker opened her mouth and he gestured. "It is okay."

Ms. Baker quickly huddled with her staff.

"Move all the residents to the other side of the hallway. They should not witness the body on the way to the morgue. These frazzled minds can shatter. I am sure they will know he died if they see the body after post mortem care."

Charles, Mirna, Dolores, and Dr. Ephraim hoisted up the dead man. Dr. Ephraim pronounced him before the emergency crew arrived. Ralph met them at the lobby and redirected them at Dr. Ephraim's request.

"Let Hal go in peace."

Dr. Ephraim spoke with the state trooper who arrived before the ambulance. Constance stood at the end of the hallway. She could see Dr. Ephraim and the policeman face to face, their gestures, and the paperwork being signed. Dr. Ephraim shook his head as he left.

Dr. Ephraim was glad he was at Whispering Pines when the staff found Hal unresponsive. The staff was adamant he had no signed DNR. They wanted to continue CPR.

Knowing Hal Blum for more than four years made it easier to make a decision as his doctor. While signing the death certificate and calling Albany to report the death, Dr. Ephraim wished that if his patients passed on, they did so without pain. No suffering, no torment, just as if they were falling asleep peacefully.

Hal had the perfect happy ending. Dr Ephraim sighed, closed his office door, and walked to his car. All the while, he was meticulously swirling his car key on his right index finger.

Elizabeth Mann approached the social worker and asked, "What happens to Hal now?"

"Well, he has no money left in his account. There are no family or friends listed. Since there are no donations available, we'll see what happens."

Elizabeth Mann picked up a large postmortem kit from the top corner shelf in the supply closet. She came up to help Mirna and Dolores. Liz knew that this was part of their job, and Hal wouldn't be the last. They tended to the body with respect and empathy as if he was still their beloved Hal.

CHAPTER 18

Anthony stood patiently by the limousine door, dressed in his black suit. His professional blank stare did not shed light into what he was thinking. Behind his dark shades, his mind wondered about the path life takes us on and what happens at the end. Being at a funeral stirs hidden emotions, rational and irrational thoughts in people. He thought about his wife and daughter.

Constance saw Anthony through the window before she went into the chapel for the service. His presence had been comforting for her at Henry's service. A sharp spasm closed her throat at the thought of Henry. She felt her eyes tearing.

Not now, hush. Hal Blum deserves all of the attention today, she chided herself harshly. *Move on, your time to mourn for yourself is not now.*

Constance had her lawyer, Ed Cohen, write a check to Anthony to make arrangements for Hal's funeral because no one else would. He died with no family and no money. His life was a mystery to all. No one ever knew the real Hal. Constance had always liked Hal and felt that the Vietnam veteran who served his country deserved a proper goodbye.

Constance entered the chapel. She stood next to the residents sitting in wheelchairs. Ruth Fisher was trying in vain to get out of the wheelchair. Francine stood next to her with her hands on her shoulders, occasionally rubbing her mother-in-law's shoulders to calm her.

Constance smiled at Francine. After her failed attempt to stand, Ruth concentrated on unlocking the wheels. Her trembling hands failed her, but she kept at it.

Is she aware she is at a funeral service? Is that why she is restless? Unable to talk and shed tears, she is restless, the only emotion her saggy face can portray.

Maria stood in a black dress with a white collar. Her hair was done. Someone, fair chance it was a volunteer, had dolled up her face. Maria's lips, covered in red lipstick, quivered. Rabbi Menachem, leading the service, motioned to the Chaplin, Fr. Sebastian to step forward to the pulpit.

Fr. Sean, Danny, and his wife, Molly, stood next to Maria. Maria moved her Rosary beads mechanically, the way she had for more than seventy-three years. She never said the prayers anymore. When she moved her Rosary beads in her right hand with her eyes closed, her face embodied the grace of a nun immersed in prayer in a cloistered nunnery.

Fr. Sean thought, *Yes, her life was a life of service to others, family and her students, and she lived her life giving up her desires. Yes, she lived for everyone around her.*

Did she get the credit she deserved? Fr Sean sighed in exhaustion.

The casket was wheeled to the front of the chapel. It was an ivory casket, with gold handles and the American flag draped over it. A proper farewell salute to a life spent on earth defending freedom for others without being able to defend himself from the demons that tormented his golden years.

"I thought he was poor. Where did he get the money for the funeral?" Anise Meyer, who worked in accounting with access to his financial status, mumbled to the lady from human resources, who shrugged her shoulders in response. They worked in offices and only passed by some of the residents by chance in the lobby.

The casket was closed after the early viewing. Anise was disappointed she had not come down early to find out who Mr. Blum was. She couldn't put a face to the name. Maybe she might have sat with him or his beloved ones and discussed options for admission and payments, or maybe she had passed him in the lobby. It could be one of the wanderers who occasionally ends up in her office.

The horrendous smell of death lingered in the air. The

pungent scent of incense and candles emitting the aura of gloom in the chapel was deemed perverse and frightening to many.

Or is it the atmosphere of celebration for the passing era of one's life and the arrival of the new journey?

It was a solemn gathering to bid farewell to Mr. Blum, a man with no family or loved ones present at his service.

Did he even have any? Maybe he never remembered any of them. Maybe they forgot him altogether. Whatever it is, today he is an honoree with a chapel full of people. Was he content with the life he chose?

Maria looked at the casket. Although the casket is closed now, she had seen him earlier: Mr. Blum dressed in a black tuxedo. His clean-shaven face, his frozen lips yearning to say, "Goodbye friends, you are my family. I am amazed at the way you care for me. I will miss you all. See ya."

Dolores stood vigilantly next to Maria. Any unusual trigger could make Maria agitated, but Maria was quiet. As the Rabbi recited Psalm 23, the chapel resonated the solemnness of the occasion.

Fr Sebastian eulogized the life of Mr. Blum in profound words.

Dolores and Maria walked behind the casket, alongside Danny, Fr. Sean, and Molly.

Handsome men dressed impeccably in long black coats and shiny shoes carried the casket to the hearse. The door was opened, and they slid the soldier in with the utmost respect. As the hearse rolled down the winding path from Whispering Pines, Maria winced as if she had a genuine thought. She turned to Dolores and stared at her as if she knows what is happening. Maybe she had a spark of reality within a lost moment. She mumbled,

The Carriage held but just ourselves-
And immortality
We slowly drove - He knew no haste
And I had put away
My labor and my leisure too,
For His Civility-

We passed the school, where Children strove
At Recess - in the Ring -
We passed the Fields of Gazing Grain -
We passed the Setting Sun -
Or rather - He passed Us -
The Dews drew quivering and Chill -
For only Gossamer, my Gown -
My Tippet - only Tulle -

Fr. Sean turned in his seat and said, "Emily Dickenson."

Molly Said, "Don't irritate her. Let her be."

Maria drifted off to a nap. She closed her eyes and eventually leaned on Dolores. She is in her safe haven unaware of any disturbing thoughts. At this moment, she did not conceive what was going on around her in the quiet of forgetfulness and exhaustion.

The pines on the sides of the winding path whispered, "Goodbye Mr. Hal Blum. You were dear to us."

The April wind waved its goodbyes and the weeping willows twirled in unison.

As the funeral procession slowly exited the winding path, the gray walls opened up to the blazing lights of an ambulance carrying the next resident.

TO MY BELOVED READERS

I hope I was able to paint a realistic picture to one of life's realities.

I dedicate the book to all of you – who ride along as one -suffering from Dementia, a caretaker, a family member, a loved one, a dear friend or an onlooker.

The journey you are on is difficult – a path filled with obstacles

Do not be discouraged. Look for moments you could cherish even if they are short lived,

Like a firefly, light up the short-lived moments.

Laugh when you can.

Reinforce negatives with positives.

Hold tight to good memories and help create new ones.

Keep your eyes open.

Dive deep- and collect the best shells.

There is Hope in every situation

Let us all hope together

Next time as you pass by remember a smile, a gentle gesture can fill a desperate heart with HOPE.

Love

Gigi

Made in the USA
Middletown, DE
06 October 2022